junIor

junIor

a novel

DISCARD

~~Macaulay Culkin~~

miramax books

HYPERION

NEW YORK

ISBN 1-4013-5234-0

First Edition
10 9 8 7 6 5 4 3 2 1

Knock-knock.
Who's there?
Junior.
Junior who?
Exactly.

QUESTIONNAIRE

ARE YOU THE "RIGHT" KIND OF READER?

Halt. Stop right where you are. You're not going to be let in that easily. How do I know you're not some kind of spy or something? How can I be sure you're honest and open-minded and accepting of what you're about to experience?

Not just anyone can read. Sure, there are illiterate people in the world and those not exposed to the craft, but that's not what I'm talking about. Through trial and massive error, Junior (meaning I) has realized that this is not an easy book to read, and should not be read by just anybody. So in an attempt to weed out the weak and ill-equipped readers, Junior has put together this list of simple questions. Be honest. They're multiple choice to make it easier on you.

You will find the answers on the following page. But don't look because that would be cheating and defeat the purpose of such an exercise.

One wrong answer and you're out of the game. Put down your book and get to the back of the line.

You have one minute.

Begin.

1. If you had to choose, would you be:

A.) A brown cow
B.) A traditional black and white cow
C.) Not a cow

answer: _____

2. When making macaroni and cheese from a box, should you:

A.) Do exactly what the directions tell
     you to do
B.) Add extra milk
C.) Use no milk at all fearing
     retaliation from the cows in question
     one

answer: _____

3. Black is:

A.) A race of people on the planet Earth
B.) The color of death
C.) Not a color

answer: _____

4. When faced with a problem in your family, you:

A.) Ignore it as usual
B.) Seek professional assistance
C.) Fucking deal with it

answer: _____

5. If your author could take something back, would it be:
A.) The time I counted to a million
B.) Professional wrestling
C.) All those lesbians
D.) The time I threw a glass at someone who tried to talk to me
E.) All the letters I should never ever send
F.) Money
G.) Trying
H.) Sleeping too much
I.) All the apologies I've ever made in my entire life
J.) This book
K.) Watching *Singing in the Rain* fifty times straight
L.) Monsters
M.) Taking a swing-dancing lesson

N.) Bathing
O.) Turning left when I should have turned right
P.) Dying my hair red
Q.) Picking up smoking
R.) Not recycling
S.) Getting drunk and telling too many stories
T.) Never forming a band
U.) Pixies
V.) Unprotected sex with strangers
W.) Dictionaries
X.) Falling off my rocking horse when I was four and cracking my head open
Y.) Eating a frog's leg
Z.) None of the above

answer: _____

Answers: 1. C
          2. C
          3. C
          4. C
          5. Z

READING RULES

Assuming you've passed the test and are ready to move on, it's time to lay down the rules. To enhance your pleasure and to protect you from any damage that these words may inflict, I have devised this simple series of rules to be followed while enjoying this piece of work. These are to be taken quite seriously and are only here for your safety. Please note that you may need to refer to this page in the future, so don't be afraid to dog-ear the corner of it along the dotted line provided above.

RULE #1: There are no rules.

RULE #2: Disregard rule #1.

RULE #3: The author does not necessarily agree with all the statements made in this book. So do not read too deeply into the true meaning of his words.

RULE #4: The writer is a serious person and should be thought of in that way. He would like to warn you not to take him or his words lightly. There is a message to his madness, if you care to listen.

RULE #5: Drink orange juice, because it's good for you.

RULE #6:

RULE #7: Imaginary, not inflatable, women are okay.

RULE #8: Your hero is the most selfish person he knows. He's competitive as well, which makes this much worse since now he wants to be the best jerk he can be. So don't be embarrassed if you have to turn away from this accident when it's at its most gruesome. Sometimes I wish I could do the same thing.

RULE #9: Your author would like to take this time to thank you for reading this far into the book. He also wants to express that he likes you very, very much and from now on you are all his friends. This isn't a rule so much as it is a chance to give back to my audience.

RULE #10:

RULE #11: You are all not going to laugh at me. (No matter what my brother says.)

RULE #12: See rule #1.

RULE #13: Junior does not know who he is, but he's rounded up the usual suspects.

You are now all much stronger and better-prepared readers. You may continue.

junIor

THE INTRODUCT-ION.

NowHere Near Nowhere.

I want to make one thing clear before we begin: I am not a writer. I couldn't possibly be a writer. I have written and rewritten the words "Introduction" or "The Introduction" so many times in the past couple of years that I'm convinced I was not born to do this. Writing could not be my calling after the mess I've made of all this. This has taken way too long. The whole process of writing this book was so agonizing and ate away at so much of my time that there's no way I can't

1

finish now. But at this rate I never will. It took me ten minutes to write this very sentence. I'm no writer. This is not my calling.

Why is it so difficult now? This used to be a comforting thing. Writing this book was fun. It made me feel better. I'm not comfortable right now. I've never felt comfortable explaining the way that I am. This (the newest in a long line of introductions) is already a failure and I've barely begun. Here I am, only on the second paragraph, and I already feel like I'm blowing it.

It's just that in the past year I have gotten way too many people involved in this project—agents, publishers and so forth that I feel I've been disappointing with my lack of results. I'm just ready to let this go. I'm just ready to give up and say this is it and nothing more. You can have it because I have nothing left.

Not in any kind of painful way, but it's hard for me to talk about this project. It's just that I don't know what it is anymore. I could just be imagining this, but people see this book in different ways. I could show this book to ten different people and have them form very different opinions of what it is and what it means to them. Sometimes I feel like I have a dozen different people inside of me. I've always been that way and I've always written stuff down. But this is different, this is the introduction of my book. I can't just wing it.

My real problem is that after a while I decided to save this introduction for last. I figured that one of the reasons this intro was so hard to write was because I needed the book and all its parts to be in place before trying to sum it all up. And to be quite honest with you, most of the material in this book is foreign to me now.

If I wanted to be all David Copperfield about it, I could say I began this project more than two decades ago on a hot summer day in a New York City hospital, but the truth is I only became of aware of it actually becoming a book in early January of 2001. It is now crawling to the end of 2005 with the completion of this endeavor nowhere in sight. So much of it was written so long ago that I may have lost sight of what it meant, not only to the reader, but to me as well. Perhaps that is why I have found it so difficult to introduce this part of myself to the

3

rest of the world, because I don't know what
it means to me anymore.

So much has changed since I first sat down
and began to write this book. I've changed. I
got arrested recently and to be quite honest
with you it wasn't as much fun as I thought it
would be. I got a new dog and I named her
Audrey. I found a girl (a real girl) that I'm
in love with, and if you can believe it, she
loves me back.

I'm looking at her right now, in fact.
She bought me a new computer and on the
desktop there's this picture of her on the
beach. She and I and a bunch of our friends
went to Hawaii recently. I had never been
there before and I enjoyed myself very much.
We had a house right on the beach. A couple of
days into it, while sitting in the shade nurs-
ing my new sunburn, she decided to try surfing
for the first time. And needless to say it was
quite a funny sight. If you've never seen
someone take their first surfing lesson
before, then drop this book and everything
else you're doing immediately and arrange it.
It's well worth it. On one of her many tumbles
into the ocean a friend of ours must have
snapped a picture of her. Her butt is on the
board as she's washing ashore and she has this

smile on her face. It looks like you've just surprised a five-year-old with a truck full of candy. I'm talking ear to ear. Every time I turn on my computer and I see this picture it makes me happy. I know how lucky I am to have someone that makes me feel that way, believe me. I'm lucky to have her.

My point is I didn't have her or that picture when I started making this book. (I may have had other pictures, but that's a different book altogether.) I didn't have a lot of things I do today. I was just some twenty-year-old punk kid who thought he could just whip out some book when I started writing this. Now I'm a twenty-four-year-old accused felon with a dog that shits all over my house and a girlfriend that can't surf. I can't account for that person or what he wrote four years ago. I can't remember his intentions.

So I've decided (just now in fact) that I'm going to disassociate myself from this book completely. I think it's the right thing to do. Too many of the people around me are scared of it, and rightfully so. I've put my words in a position to be easily misinterpreted and used against me. So from now on this is not my book. Understood?

Maybe some visual aids will help us both.

This is me.

And this is my book.

Get it?

6

Me.

My book.

There, I think that helped us both
better understand that this is my book and not
me. This isn't even a proper representation of
the way I feel at this very moment. This is
just a collection of words put together in a
way of my choosing to tell some kind of story.
So from now on nothing you read (including
this introduction) is my fault, it's the
book's fault.

See how I got myself off the hook? A real writer wouldn't have done that. I am not a writer. I am a fraud, and you can quote me on that. I can read the headlines now. "Young man uses connections to get book published." The reviews nearly write themselves. In fact, I wouldn't be very surprised if these last couple of sentences are the most quoted of any other. I'm a sham, a fraud, and a failure all at the same time. And this introduction proves it.

One of the things I hate most about this book is that it is all about me. Much like anyone with too much time on his or her hands, I feel as though I am the most important person on earth and everything I do is relevant. I say the most charming and inspired things when no one is around. I think I might have something to say and that everyone in the entire world wants to know about it.

Almost everything people do is artistic. That doesn't make it art. I may be being too hard on myself but that is the reality of my world and I'm letting you know how aware of it I really am. I'm not trying to pass this book off as something it is not. This is just a bunch of stuff I put together and someone said

8

"Hey, you should write a book," so I did. It might not be your cup of tea. You might only get a couple pages into it and throw it in the trash. You might not even give yourself a chance to read this very sentence.

But who knows, you could be one of the people out there who might actually like it. You may be able to say all the things about it I can't say for myself. But then again, I'm not a writer.

So here it comes, the book. You can say anything you want about it now. It's not mine anymore.

the end . . .

blank

THE
END.

part one

the end of me.

EXCERPTS FROM MY UNFINISHED MEMOIR TITLED *THE LIFE AND TIMES OF MONKEY-MONKEY BOY*

Pg. 2

As I sit down and begin to write what could be called my life story, I would like to remind the reader that many of the things that happened to me in my life, or at least those found interesting enough to write about, happened to me at a very early age. So if I don't have my stories straight, or if I indulge the facts, or freely jump forwards and backwards in time, don't be taken off-guard. My life as I know it and my life as you knew it are two totally different things.

SCENE MISSING

Pg. 8

. . . my only solace comes from the fact that by the time anyone reads this most of the people involved will probably be dead.

SCENE MISSING

Pg. 55

. . . and that's when the staring began. I remember quite clearly when it first started. I was on leave from the circus and spending time with my brothers. We were sitting in a room somewhere in Florida playing video games when something caught my eye. In the window, a face. It quickly bobbed out of sight. I thought nothing of it and continued playing. But it came again and this time it was unmistakable. It wasn't just one face, it was three. Three kids my age standing at our window. I caught the first glimpse of the look on their faces that I have now grown to recognize. Their eyes in a daze and jaws open in typical comic-book fashion, they ducked out of sight and ran and laughed with excitement. By the time my brothers and I dropped our controllers and got to the window to see what had happened, the kids were on their bikes riding away from us as fast as they could.

Then it clicked. I knew those kids. I had seen them before, around the neighborhood. I didn't know their names but I knew them. We had mutual friends. We used to be the same.

From that point on I knew everything was going to be different. There was a different set of rules that applied to me.

SCENE MISSING

Pg. 98

"CLUCK! CLUCK!" They yelled at the top of their lungs. The entire group of photographers, three or four deep, chanted this as I made my way through the press line of my newest circus act in New York. I knew what they wanted because I had given it to them so many times before that I lost count (not that I was counting). I could barely make out what they were saying under the sea of voices.

"Hey, hey Monkey Boy! Look over here," I heard from one of the desperate ones in the back.

"Yo Monkey Boy, do that thing you do. Do that clucking like a chicken thing," said another.

13

But in the front there seemed to be one photographer in particular who I thought was high on speed or just plain crazy. He kept on yelling "CLUCK! CLUCK! CLUCK!" until his voice became raspy and hoarse. His face was so red I thought it was going to explode.

I had been to dozens of my own premieres before. It was supposed to be old hat by then, but there was something wrong that night, something in the air. Then suddenly everything began to spin and it became increasingly hard to breathe. They were yelling so loud I couldn't even think. The flashes from the cameras were so bright I couldn't even see.

In a moment like that, when you're thirteen years old, you're not thinking "I'm having a panic attack"; your instinct is to flee. Run, get out of there as soon as you can before a hole opens up beneath your feet and the world swallows you up. So I did what my gut was telling me to do: I ran. No matter what people were going to think, no matter how unprofessional it was, I didn't care. I had to get out of there at that very moment.

The crowd's reaction was less than sympathetic, to say the least. The moment I reached the lobby of the theatre, before I could catch my breath, a chorus of boos and jeers could be heard from outside. The photographers were obviously not happy with my swift and abrupt exit and were letting the rest of the world know

14

about it. I didn't care about them. My thoughts were all about self-preservation, not my career or the career of some lowly paparazzo.

Then it hit me like a wave: shame. I began to scan the crowd and noticed a couple of friendly faces, people whom I had invited to my big night. Family, friends, everyone was listening to the wave of boos coming from outside my own premiere. How could *I* let that happen? How could they do that in front of everyone on my night?

Just then I got a tap on the shoulder. It was a young woman from the publicity department of the New York City circus. "I think you should go back out there," she whispered in my ear.

Of course not, I thought. I can't give them anything after the way they treated me, the way they embarrassed me in front of everyone. I don't have to give them anything.

Just then I got another tap on the shoulder. It was my father. He didn't say a word to me but I knew what he wanted. He commanded me, with his eyes, to go back out there. It was my job to go back out there.

So I lowered my head, picked up my tail and headed out the door. The mob of photographers didn't cheer when I returned, of course. They just yelled, "Do that chicken dance, monkey boy!" and I obliged, knowing that they were killing any speck of joy I used to have for my work.

I'll never forget that night and what I learned

15

from it. Shame on them for doing that. Shame on me
for letting them get away with it.

SCENE MISSING

Pg. 126

. . . and it was right about this time that I began
reassessing my life and trying to figure out what
kind of relationship I wanted to have with my
family.

With my stint as Monkey-Monkey Boy behind
me, and all my memories from that era now in-
voluntarily erased from my mind, I realized that this
was an opportunity for me. This was not a curse at all;
this was a blessing. I was in that rarest of positions
where I could redefine my life as I wanted it to be. I,
for the first time in my life, could make decisions for
myself that were solely for my benefit. My universe re-
volved around me.

The machine, the industry, that grew around
Monkey-Monkey Boy was so large and the pressures so
great that it suffocated any sense of self. People's liveli-
hoods were on the line and I couldn't let them down.
And not in the "Rah rah, team spirit" kind of way but
the "Fail and I'll hurt you" way that reduced me to a
robotlike state. It drove me into my shell.

A long time I spent in random hotel rooms

around the world thinking about how life could be. But now I was free. I was fourteen years old and free to decide what kind of life I wanted.

SCENE MISSING

Pg. 203

I needed time to reflect. I was getting older and so much had happened in such a short amount of time that I didn't have the chance to think; I didn't let myself. This was about the time that I began writing these memoirs, but I thought that was lame. The mere thought that someone could retire at fourteen is silly enough, but to presume that my life warranted publishing a memoir at twenty seemed absolutely absurd. So I dropped the entire project and began a new one . . .

A TOAST
Here is a toast to lovers lost. To friends and family reborn and a newfound life to be lived. Here's to decisions made, mistakes made, remade, regretted, and retracted again. To things lost and things never to be found. To the joys of life and to traumas thankfully avoided. Here's to thought, and to sleepless

nights haunted by such things. Here's to the
initial blast of cold water I get hit with in
the shower every morning. Here is to the
prospect of future love. Here's to me, and
the twenty years it took me to be able to say
that. Here is to the end of my toast.

cornelius and the beanstalk.

I am a collection of thoughts and
memories and likes and dislikes. I am the
things that have happened to me and the sum of
everything I've ever done. I am the clothes
I wear on my back. I am every place and every
person and every object I have ever come
across. I am a bag of bones stuck to a very
large rock spinning a thousand miles an hour. I
am nonsense. I am the grand total of everything
I have and everything I have never been exposed
to, but you don't know that. You don't know
that because you don't know me . . . or is it
the other way around? And if you don't know me,
or anything about me, then why should you
continue on? Why go any further? Otherwise I'm
just feeding you shit.

THE FOLLOWING WAS A REPORT FILED BY JUNIOR
FOR A SENIOR ART PROJECT FOR A CLASS TITLED
"REBELS AND VISIONARIES."

HE RECEIVED A C—.

it doesn't matter how you cook it

by: junior

22

23

25

moral

it doesn't matter how you cook it...

if people are hungry enough, they'll eat shit and like it

end.

I'VE NEVER BEEN TO THE MOON

When I was a young boy, no more than four years old, my father used to take me to work with him, which was an absolute thrill for me because he worked in a church. I used to love to help him clean the organ or ring the big bells in the big bell tower. And on one of those days when I had the privilege of going to work with him, I asked him if I could go to the moon. It must have been funny to him because he laughed. So I asked him again, and again and again and again. You have to understand that this was a serious question and he wasn't taking me seriously. I must have asked him a thousand and one times and was either laughed at or ignored. But by the thousand and second time I said "I wanna go the mooooon," he finally said yes.
I've never been to the moon.

CHECKPOINT

So far you have read 461 words and 1,787 individual letters.

THE WEMBLING WARRIOR Part 56

I am the knight of knights. I am the king of kings. I am the reason for everything that is and the end-all be-all of beef jerky. I am the hokey pokey of Manchester blondes. I had sex with a waitress one time. I am the Wembling Warrior and I am that I am . . . the breakfast of champions.

My nineteen favorite movies:
The Godfather part I. The Graduate. Breakfast at Tiffany's. Rushmore. Taxi Driver. Dr. Strangelove. Amadeus. Brazil. Raising Arizona. One Flew Over the Cuckoo's Nest. The Hudsucker Proxy. Harold and Maude. Network. Zero Effect. The Sting (only the first time I watched it). *CQ. Babe. Pulp Fiction. Midnight Cowboy.*

SELF IMAGE
biglipscrookednoseoneeyebiggerthantheother

A FASHIONABLE YOUNG MAN
I am a boy. I am a beautiful boy. I am only skin deep. I am a Burberry bird. I am a Prada penguin. I am the Hiawatha of lake Gichi Gucci. And a Versace jalopy. The skins I wear to school every day.

DEAR GOD

Dear god,

Why is everything wrong?

Love,

Oscar de la Mancha

I WATCH TELEVISION

5 . . . 4 . . . 3 . . . 2 . . .
Ladies and gentlemen, I . . . watch . . .
television. Which doesn't mean a lot to me,
but it sure means a lot to everyone else. When
I was younger than I am today I watched T.V.
and I liked it very much, so I kept watching.
So some don't bother me. Others dismiss me as
lazy. Like I'm not worth the food I eat or the
bed I sleep in. Like I don't exist because I
haven't cured some disease or invented a hilar-
ious refrigerator alarm. But I don't care. I
keep watching because I like to watch. I just
wish there was nothing expected of me and no
one cared where I was. I don't exist. Years
later I became a traveler. There I am traveling
to the kitchen and there I am traveling to the
bathroom. And throughout my many adventures

to places unknown, I have truly learned
absolutely nothing. Which means I have learned
more than I think I have and I'm worth more
then I give myself credit for. But what is
that worth? Certainly not my weight in gold,
which brings me to another point: How do we
know we really exist? Is the fact that I'm
standing here enough to prove that I'm really
here? Like if a tree falls in the woods, would
anyone hear me? So if an alien race lands on
the planet Earth tomorrow and asks me to prove
I'm really here, what do I do? What do I give
them? What do I tell them? What do I show
them? I can't sing or dance. I can't paint.
I've never built anything and I've never
contributed anything significant to the human
race. Like I was never here and no one would
miss me if I were gone.

But I do have a family, and I do have friends,
and so-called friends, and acquaintances, and
many other people I see only around Christmas
time. Maybe they could vouch for me. Maybe
they could testify to my existence and save a
part of me that thinks I'm no better than a
bag of potato chips.

So who am I? Now that I'm here, how do I
measure my worth? You could say the

collection of meager possessions I have gath-
ered over the course of my short life is who
I am. Is what a man owns who he is? I have a
gorilla named Abe. Is that who I am? Is that
how I'll be remembered?

I hope not. I hope I'm remembered as the king
of the world, the noble man who united all
the nations of the earth. But that probably
won't happen. At least not to me and
definitely not today, because today I'm going
to do what I do every day: I'm going to sit
in bed and exist. I will do nothing and have
nothing to show for it. Put most simply, in
the words of my beloved Popeye: "I am what I
am and that is all that I am." And that is
how I exist.

I . . . watch . . . television.

MY NAZI FRIEND
I have a friend who talks a lot about Hitler.
I don't think he's a Nazi, he just likes to be
looked at.

Eat me. Drink me.

Right now beans cost $1.99 a pound.

It is shocking and surprising but not totally unexpected.

I call my little brother a doppelganger just to hear him say "What's a doppelganger?"

DAD—Part 1
One could say that my father was a loving man who looked out for the best interests of his family. In fact, that's what he said. But others would say that he was a cold-blooded bastard who ripped my family apart from the inside out. I say he was what he was and no one could ever change that. To start, I think my father did do everything he could to secure my family's future. He fought like a tiger. He fought the way a man should against his enemies. But he had too many enemies. Some I could never see. He had invisible enemies.

Honey dew.
Money do.
Think the things I think I think . . .
I think.
But not for a living.

FOLLOWERS
To be the same as all the others is to be the
wine I drink every night. You are the reason
my blood doesn't clot.

THE TRUTH ABOUT PURPLE LIONS
One day a small boy asked me, "Are there
purple lions?" as he colored a picture of one
of them. I had to think about this for a long
time. I wondered if it would be wrong to lie
to him and say "Yeah sure, purple lions are
everywhere" or if I should just give it to him
straight and say "no." What is a man to say?

LOOK WHAT I KNOW
Did you know the largest artery in the human
body is the aorta? Did you know Muhammad is
the most common name in the world? Did you
know the name "Wendy" did not exist before the
book *Peter Pan* was published? Did you know the
Bible is the best-selling book in the world?
Did you know Harvey Fierstein is gay? Did you
know 40% of American high school students cannot locate Canada on a map? Did you know the
capital of Luxemburg is Luxemburg? Did you
know I have a pet name for my penis (Floyd)?

Did you know one in three people believes
plastic is an essential part of life? Did you
know 70% of people believe in life after
death? Did you know seven out of ten people
think Babe Ruth is the all-time home-run champion? Did you know Hank Aaron is the all-time
home-run champion? Did you know Babe Ruth is
white? Did you know Eskimos have 49 words for
snow? Did you know most people from Fargo do
not like the movie *Fargo?* Did you know
Greenland was once named Iceland and Iceland
was once called Greenland? It's true. Did you
know the Vikings did that to keep people away
from their green land? Did you know . . .

a monkey
and if you read this

time and space.

BAM

I want to burn a Y onto everyone's forehead.

I want to be able to hump people's legs and
have them do nothing about it.

Humpty dumpty and his false relations.

34

I keep one of my best friends in a jar.

THE PEOPLE I LIKE THE LEAST (in no particular order) . . .

████████████████████████████████████

Dad. ████████ Jerry Falwell. General
Pinochet. George W. Bush. Kenny G. Mark David
Chapman. Dennis Rodman. Everyone who takes
acting awards seriously. Hitler. Sinéad
O'Connor. Blah. Marg Schott. Doctors. Non-
drinkers. People who wear too much leather.
People who wear too much cologne. X-man Rogue.
Lawrence Phillips. All my sisters' boyfriends.
Paparazzi. Stupid people. Vanilla Ice. X-Pac.
Alcoholics. Vegans. Joseph Jackson. People
I love who don't love me back. My dad's
girlfriend(s). People who eat raw leeks.
People who make too much noise when they chew.
████████████████████ Pete Sampras. People who
eat too much curry. People who attend Limp
Bizkit concerts. Deadheads. People who cannot
control their sex drives. Bill Maher. ████
████████████████████. People who
read too many magazines. ████████. Wonder
Woman. People who seek therapy over the Inter-
net. People who whisper too much. Unfunny people. James Toback. ████. People who are small

35

minded. People who tell me their life story within ten minutes of meeting them. People from Texas. ███████████████████████. People who go on the Jerry Springer show and act surprised when something horrible happens. People who wear digital watches. People who keep their cell phones on all the time. People who cough and do not cover their mouths. Rapists. People who enjoy masturbating too too much. The 1994 Houston Rockets. The 1999 San Antonio Spurs. ████████████████████████. People who have too many cats. Tony Schiavone. Republicans and Democrats. People who read the *Enquirer* and the *Star*. Andrea Pizer. People who flip out over a bug. J. Edgar Hoover. The people who put "to be continued" on my T.V. screen. People who believed in manifest destiny. Walt Disney. People who like me too quickly. Junior. Murderers. Autograph hounds. Robin Givens. The people who cancelled *The Snorks*. Judd Nelson (post—*Breakfast Club*). People who sunbathe regularly. People who sell heroin. Copernicus. Anyone who does not think Audrey Hepburn is beautiful. ██████████████ ████████████████████████. Christopher Columbus. James Earl Ray. Opinionated people.

I like putting folk music where it's not
wanted.

Brett is an asshole.

DAD—PART 2
My father used to pace. He would walk from one
end of our small apartment to the other all
day long. He used to twitch his fingers and
talk to himself for hours on end. When I was
young and naïve I asked my father why he used
to pace and twitch his fingers and talk to
himself. He told me it was the coffee. He said
he drank too much coffee and the caffeine made
him do these things. I took him at his word
and never wondered why everyone else who drank
coffee didn't do the same thing. I told him he
should stop drinking coffee. He drank more.
My father liked to drink things other than
coffee. Sometimes he would give me a sip of
what he was having. He loved Bloody Mary's.
They were a little too spicy for my taste.

Fabulous!

Zooty bang.

Eclectic. Erratic. Eccentric.

I don't know what the word "urban" means
anymore.

I don't know what I'm doing.

I see the sun
And say hello
The sun will soon be here tomorrow

SPACES IN WRONG PLACES
Igo tsp ace s inw rong pla cesl ike a bo ywi
thn o bra ces,lik e a crow d w it hn ofac es,l
ik e ac op wi th no c a s es.

I g otspac es inwron g p l aceslik ea ca rwi t
hn orace s, li k e aba llw ith nob ase s, l ik
e a d eck wit h n o ac es.

Ig ot sp a ce s inwro ngp la ces lik e a mov I
ewi th n och as es,likea me al wi thno g ra
ces, l ik e a flow er w it hn ov as e s.

I g o tspac es inwrongpl a c esl ike a p
honewithn o trac es, lik e a sh o ewith nol
aces, a n d aprea cher w ithn o pr ais es.

I go tsp a c esi n wr o ng p l ac es.

Slip and slide

Superman

Peter Panhandle

Why are men scared of ballet but absolutely
head over heels about wrestling?

SEVENTEEN PROVERBS
1. kill two birds with one stone. 2. don't
shit where you sleep. 3. you can pick your
nose but you can't pick your family. 4. let
sleeping dogs lie. 5. don't let the bedbugs
bite. 6. one bad apple spoils the bunch. 7.
life is like a box of chocolates etc. 8.
every cloud has a silver lining. 9. a bird in
the hand is worth two in the bush. 10. don't
look a gift horse in the mouth. 11. honest
money goes further. 12. there's more than one
way to skin a cat. 13. an eye for an eye, a
tooth for a tooth. 14. the early bird catches
the worm. 15. if at first you don't succeed,
try try again. 16. it all comes out in the
wash. 17. the past is the past. the present
is the present. and the future is the past.

CORNELIUS AND THE
BEANSTALK (Continued . . .)

So now you know a lot more than you did
before. But there may be something beyond the
surface. What is Junior all about? And what if
my name wasn't Junior? What if I've been lying
to you all this time? What if my real name was
Rueben Hasenpfeffer III? Would that make
everything I just told you any less true?
But what if I'm approaching this all wrong?
You don't need anything. You don't need me to
tell you anything at all. Do you think you
would know the story of Jack and the beanstalk
if Jack's name were Cornelius? Or Jamal?

junior = old man.

FORWARD

There's no way home. I blew the bridge.
There's nowhere to go but forward. One foot in
front of another. I hope I can remember that.
The whole foot thing. It's all a blur now. I
cried about a steak sandwich one time. But it
wasn't really about a steak sandwich. I don't
know what it was, but no cow has that power
over me. Did I miss what was? Did I try to run
back to the ashes? Second thoughts. Tears
flowing over nothing. Making mountains. Building a new home with my bare hands. Running
some more. I like to skwoosh bugs. I like
looking at the things that disgust people.
It's too foggy to see one of man's greatest
creations. Maybe the next time I pass through
I may lay eyes on things worth looking at. I
felt bad for the devil one time. His wife had
thrown all his things on the front lawn. He,
as usual, had done something evil, something
human. His spectacles were all twisted and
smashed, all of his clothes had grass stains
on them, and she even left a broken suitcase
for him to take his things away in. I felt bad

for a heartbeat. But then I thought
(remembered) that he was the devil, and he
probably deserved it. That bastard. Crossroads
of life. No time to turn around. Nothing to
see anyway. Did you (I) take a wrong turn
somewhere? Oh well, no time to think. Just
keep moving. Getting friendly with a stranger.
Life is weird. Things you say. Things said to
you. Feeling stupid now. Should I pop another
bottle? I'm a maniac you know, I go pop all
the time. Just don't fall in love with me. So
easy to say, right? Can't turn around now.
Gotta keep going. Don't (remember) forget to
feed the cats. All of them. In the whole wide
world. And don't forget to do the shopping. I
need spinach and tampons. And I need you to
pick up the dry cleaning. And pay the bills.
And take out the garbage. And draw up your
will . . . thank god I can't turn around. I
better move on. I like crossing things out. I
make lists just to make check marks. I am not
the best. I get bored sometimes. My chest is a
faucet. Good to the last drop. A well has run
dry. Uninspiring kisses. Unanswered letters. I
have doubt(s). You and I would look like
fools. Faults: me/you. Probably not. I'm too
crazy. But not weird enough. And a clever fool
to boot. And there's no worse fool that I can
think of. But no (all the) time for that. I

should just move on. Don't think about her.
Don't think about her. Don't think about . . .
Where am I again? I miss understood. It's been
years since I've had that. But shit happens,
kids. You can't take anything back. You can
only say you're sorry. I'm sorry for all those
unapologetic moments that made me look like a
fool. I am only moving forward.

JUST OUT OF REACH
My twenty-first birthday is coming up soon, so
it's time to reevaluate my life. Ready?

People have to make decisions in life. That's
unavoidable. You may be able to avoid the
question for a while, like whether or not to
scratch that itch on your inner thigh, but
eventually you have to decide. You have to
make decisions.

When you get old enough or mature enough you
have to decide what you are going to do with
your life. I have done that twice. One
decision, of course, was to be a writer.
Although that just sort of happened. And the
other was to be a baker. I really wanted to be
a baker. When I was four years old I thought
it was so amazing that you could put eggs and

45

flour and chocolate or whatever into a bowl and into the oven and it becomes something. Something good. I wanted to be one of those people who made things with my hands. I went to school across the street from a bakery. I had to walk by it twice a day, both to and from school. My father was friends with the owner or head baker or whoever and he would allow my siblings and me in the back to see where they made everything. There seemed to be hundreds of ovens with thousands of tasty treats coming out of them. The baker was so nice, he would give us all the broken Christmas cookies or smooshed Halloween cupcakes or whatever seasonal sweets were on tap. And occasionally, if I had the money, I would buy a fresh chocolate éclair and begin eating it before I left the store. It would be finished before I even got to the corner.

I guess some dreams are . . . you know.

I've made only two decisions in my life.

I am going to be twenty forever.

Today is my 21st birthday
(Happy birthday Junior)

And now is officially the beginning of the end
for our young hero. Peter Pan is all grown up
now and can't come out to play anymore. As of
today, Junior is an A-dult.

DAD—PART 3
I once had a party. It wasn't my birthday or
anything but it was still important to me. My
father didn't like my friends much and called
most of them freeloaders. So rather then have a
bunch of thirteen-year-old hooligans running
around his house, he got us a hotel room, in a
very fancy hotel. He left us unsupervised. This
was to be a weekend party and my friends were
to spend two nights. The first night my friends
and I had a good time watching basketball on
T.V. and ordering way too much room service. We
spilled a drink or two and tried our best to
clean it up. And as young teenagers do, we
threw a small ball around the room and, as
expected from young teenagers, we broke a small
piece off of one of the chandeliers. There was
some roughhousing and I ended up with a
goodhearted fat lip. We all went peacefully to
sleep that night with dreams of fun had and fun
to be had the next day . . .

So it came as no surprise to me when my father
woke me up by dragging me out of bed by my

47

face. He just happened to be in the
neighborhood and stopped by. He was angry
because the room looked like a group of
teenagers had spent the night there.

But my father didn't beat me in front of
my friends, because that would have been
embarrassing. He barely yelled, because that
would have been crude. Instead he lined all
of my friends up at the front door, pulled
out his wallet, and one by one he handed
each of them a fresh twenty-dollar bill and
told them never to speak to me again.

And the kicker was they took it. All but one of
my so-called friends took the money and ran. I
was hurt. It wasn't the humiliation of being
dragged out of bed by my face that made me want
to remember. It wasn't the shame of him paying
my friends off that made the experience
painful. It was the fact that he was right. My
friends were a bunch of freeloaders who took
the money and ran. This was a test that I
didn't know I was taking, and I failed.

Of course my friends talked to me again, but I
think it was because they wanted another
twenty dollars.

GETTING OVER BEING OLDER

Now that I'm twenty-one years old and much
more mature than I was yesterday, I would
like to share with my younger audience a few
minor details that might benefit them in
their struggle to be heard. Because we all
know the more mature we are, the more people
listen. (Donkey Tracks-Apple Jacks) So here
we go.

True.
The older you get the more you sweat.

False.
You are going to be thankful for all the
things your parents did for your own good.

True.
The older I get the more I enjoy the taste of
mushrooms.

True.
Buying and drinking alcohol has virtually zero
thrill once your real I.D. becomes your really
real I.D. (so drink up children).

True.
You do not become your parents.

49

True.
You will become so nauseatingly like them you will want to puke.

True.
You do not become your parents.

False.
Cracking your knuckles will give you arthritis.

False.
Brussels sprouts are good for you.

True.
The older you get the more people refer to you by your childhood nickname.

False.
Laughing at handicapped people is cool.

True.
The older you get, the more you laugh at dirty jokes.

False.
When you get older you will have sex all the time. (Well, at least some of us will.)

False.
When you get older you will be able to do anything you want.

True.
Chicks dig a guy who knows how to shave.

So now you young people have all the
ammunition you need to succeed in the A-dult
world. I have little use for it now.

I learned how to read court papers when I was
fourteen years old . . .

the end . . .

blank

THE
END.

part two

for you

    I wrote a poem about you. Would you like to hear it? It's on my computer. It's on sleep mode. I'll just wake it up. You know I really like you. This poem is actually a part of a book written for you. Dedicated to you.

    Hold on a second. Let me just check the wire. Whoa, that scared me. I thought my computer was frozen or broken or something, but I think it's working now. You know I think about you all the time. I think about you and write stuff down. But there's this one poem I think you'd really like.

What the hell is wrong with this thing? This is like the fiftieth time my computer has broken in the last year. I should just throw this damned thing out. Do you think I'm crazy? Am I crazy in the fun-to-be-around kind of way or the mentally insane way? I love you.

i know you don't
love me.

BECAUSE OF THE PERSONAL AND PRIVATE NATURE OF THE FOLLOWING STORY, TITLED "JACK AND THE BATHROOM MISHAP," AND A CONFIDENTIALITY AGREEMENT TO THAT EFFECT, ONLY THIS PORTION CAN BE SHOWN TO YOU AT THIS TIME.

SLAM!

Time stood still. Jack thought he had locked the door. For that slightest of moments when time stopped and began again, before he even turned his head to see who it was, Jack fantasized that it would be Elaine. That perhaps she fought her way through the line of drunken strangers waiting to get into the bathroom and found some way to open the door so that she could be alone with him. Maybe she would lunge towards him with a thousand kisses and tell Jack "I love you and have loved you for all these distant years." They would leave that awful loft and that silly party and go anywhere where people wouldn't judge him if he decided to kiss her neck and tell her what he had been feeling all this time.

This could be Elaine right behind him.
Right now. This could be the beginning of what
he's secretly been asking for all this time.
What he thinks he needs for himself, the
potential disaster. He hadn't seen her in nearly
two years and it had been another two years
before that encounter. Jack had known Elaine for
more than ten years, but recently only from a
distance. Their paths would cross every once in
a while throughout their young lives but,
because of timing and circumstance, a true
relationship could never be forged. But now
everything was different, especially Jack. He
was looking to fill a gaping hole in his life.
And at that very moment where time ceased to
exist, Jack decided for sure that Elaine was the
one to fill it. There was no one else in the
world he would rather be alone in that bathroom
with than Elaine. They could run off to some
faraway island and exist purely for each other.
He would write poetry for her that she would
love and appreciate and put in a special book
where she keeps those kinds of things. Like so
many times before, he saw the two of them with
grey hair, only moderately jaded, sitting in
rocking chairs, being thoroughly satisfied with
their long lives together.
    Now granted, that's a lot for one young
man to think in one brief moment, but as only

the lucky few of you out there may know, when
your heart skips a beat, a moment like this
could last for an eternity. All the things
you've ever done in your life, all the moments
that make you cringe, all the memories that make
you smile, all the things that make you who you
are determine how you are going to act in the
moments following. You become a raw version of
yourself, stripped of the obstacles that you set
up to protect yourself. They collapse in a pile
of dust and all you're left with is yourself.
You're exposed, naked. You are uncertain of who
you are because you are unsure of what you might
do or say in that exact moment. It's like faint-
ing with your eyes open. It's like swimming
without the luxury of water. It's like dreaming
without the security of a bed.

But wait . . . What if he's getting ahead
of himself? It may have been one second, maybe
two in real time, but Jack hasn't even turned
his head yet to see who it is. Does he want it
to be her? Is he afraid that it just might be?
And what if it isn't her? What if it's some
stranger just trying to use the bathroom? C'mon
Jack, just turn your head, damn it!

"Hi," he heard over his shoulder.

Time began once more as Jack tore himself
away from the sink long enough to see who it was.
And to the complete and total surprise of Jack,

he saw Elaine standing there. Jack wasn't used to getting what he wished for, so this transition from dream to reality was a rough one for him. A thousand nights of perverted dreams came flooding back. He saw her standing there, her back against the door; she breathed through her mouth, a bit of sweat on her chest, probably from dancing all night. Although his thoughts spun around in a million different directions, Jack had enough presence of mind to utter a "hi" back at her.

There was a brief moment when the both of them just looked at each other. C'mon Jack, say something. Say something witty and smooth. Say something that will make her smile. No wait; say something that will make her think. No-no-no, disarm her with a compliment and follow with a question, that's what I was always taught. Better yet, just say something, because this awkward moment that you've created would even kill the pin before it was dropped. Say something before she begins to feel the same way. Say something before you explode.

"Having fun?" Jack said. It was better then nothing.

"Sure," she said. "Why, are you having a good time?"

"Yeah. Why not. It's better than that restaurant, right?" You could feel the beads of sweat building on the back of Jack's neck.

She nodded her head for a moment. "Right."

"What was up with that fish?" Jack continued. "It still had bones in it . . . and eyes. What's up with that?"

A pause. What's going to happen? Anything. There are a million different directions to go in and the fish eye story was less than impressive.

Should he take her off-guard and lunge right in and kiss her on the mouth with as much passion as his soul could muster? Should he be mysterious and just walk out that door and leave her standing there? Or maybe he should just lean up against the wall doing his best James Dean? But nothing in Jack's thoughts could prepare him for what happened next. Elaine, the beautiful, sexy, desirable Elaine, began pulling her pants down.

What do you do? What do you say? What could you say? Of all the things Jack was prepared for, this was not one of them.

But where is this leading? Sex . . . in the bathroom . . . in the middle of a party?

She's rather forward, isn't she? He never
thought Elaine was that kind of girl. But if
that's what she wants, who's Jack to complain
. . . right? But is this really the way he
wants to begin a relationship? Sex in the bathroom—it's something you do with sorority girls
at the alpha beta house. But, Jack considered,
I have done it in odder places and she sure
looks good tonight.

But right as Jack's libido was in full
swing, disaster. Disaster to the umpteenth
degree. Not only was Jack wrong about her intentions in the bathroom, he may have been wrong
about her intentions towards him. Elaine,
looking as good as she ever had, with her pants
down to her knees, *sat on the toilet.*

"You don't mind, do you? There's just
such a long line outside," she said, awfully
casual.

"Yeah, go right on ahead," Jack said, fum-
bling a bit.

"You've seen a girl pee before, right?"

"Sure I have," Jack said. "No big deal. I
have a couple of sisters."

See, right there is the problem. Jack is
in love with this woman and trying his best to
get her to love him back and he just compared
her to his sister. That's why you never let

girls use the bathroom in front of you unless
they are:

    A.) Your sister

    B.) Your long-term girlfriend/wife

    OR

    C.) Your buddy

Now, she was definitely, not Jack's sister
and lord knows she was not his girlfriend, so
what was Elaine trying to say?

"Would you mind turning on the water? It
helps me go," she said, disrupting his thoughts.

"Sure." Jack obliged, turning the water on
as high as it could go. It was too late to run
out the door screaming like a maniac anyway.

"Thanks," she said.

"No problem," Jack said. He's too cool.

Jack stood there until Elaine finished
what she was doing, trying his best not to look,
but also trying to look like he was not looking
at her. It was all very confusing.

Elaine finished up what she was doing and
got up. There was an odd look on her face. She
was thinking or deciding something. She walked
over to the sink and began washing her hands.
"Where do you want to go after this?" she
asked.

"I don't know. My brother's at a party
about two blocks away. I'm not sure how good it

is, but we could stop by," Jack said, a bit distracted, a bit deflated.

With her back to him, Elaine just shrugged her shoulders.

"There's an all-night diner I know about if you're hungry," Jack said, trying something else.

But this time there was no reaction from Elaine, none at all.

"I heard about this place that—" And before Jack could finish his thought, Elaine swirled around and kissed him on the mouth. A bit awkward at first, but they eventually found their rhythm. Was this the impulsive act of someone crying out for love? Was she drunk? Was she bored? If it wasn't Jack, would it have been someone else? Despite all these questions they continued to kiss. To hear Jack tell it, it lasted forever.

Slowly their lips parted and the kiss that Jack had so longed for ended. Their arms slipped around each other and Elaine and Jack just held one another. They swayed back and forth very slowly. I know for a fact that they both needed this.

Jack whispered in her ear, "I check up on you, you know."

Elaine took a deep breath and nodded. "I know. I've been checking up on you too."

They held each other some more. It could have been only ten seconds, it could have been ten minutes, it could have been an eternity. As I told you before, when your heart skips a beat, time can stand still.

KNOCK KNOCK KNOCK ! ! !

And just as easily as Elaine had fallen into his arms, she was out of them. She began fixing her hair and straightening her shirt. Jack wanted to say something. She wanted to say something. But no words were passed between the couple. They couldn't even look one another in the eye.

KNOCK KNOCK KNOCK ! ! !

That person outside the bathroom really needed to go, apparently. And so did Elaine. Before Jack had the chance to say something to her, or grab her by the arm, or just scream out, she whisked out the door. Why would she run away? Did she feel guilty for some reason? Was what they did wrong?
It sure didn't feel that way to poor Jack. He was left there in the bathroom with the door wide open. He saw the back of Elaine as she fought her way through the crowd.

65

The young man with the pseudo rock-star haircut at the front of the line, the one who was pounding away at the door, just gave Jack a scandalous smile and a wink, as if he knew what was going on in that bathroom. He may have been right.

Jack made his way through the packed hallway . . .

MISTAKES (read once, then read again slowly)
Never make the
the same mistake twice.
Never make the
the same mistake twice.

THE TALE OF OSCAR DE LA MANCHA
Oscar de la Mancha was a man of great nobility, grace, and stature. He was the king of the world and nothing could stop him until he met a girl who would take off her bras and give them to Oscar. Now, up until this time, Oscar de la Mancha was pure of heart, and his soul was as hungry as a bear after a long winter sleep. When Oscar met this woman, he forgot. He forgot everything: his family, his friends, his home, his career, his social

status. He forgot everything important in life and replaced it with her. She was his ideal. She was his everything and he forgot who he was. And when the couple got married he forgot some more. This went on for a few years until one morning Oscar woke up with whatever pieces he had left and remembered enough of himself to know he wasn't who he was, he wasn't what he wanted to be, and if he didn't act fast he could never be the man he once was and never be what he could be. So Oscar de la Mancha locked himself in his office for eternity. And just before he decided to emerge from his self-imposed exile, he took out his imaginary gun and shot himself in the foot. The wound bled for seventeen weeks. It bled a lot. It bled all over his sheets and all over his family and it bled all over his friends. But the wound healed and the bleeding stopped for Oscar de la Mancha when he met a girl who curled her tongue when they kissed . . .

A VENGEFUL CARNIVORE

I dated a vegetarian for many years. We loved each other and we hated each other. I think of the good times all the time. I remind myself of the bad as often as possible. I just got

off the phone with her. I want a cheeseburger.
With bacon. And I'm gonna have one too.

MY ALL-TIME FAVORITE QUOTE FROM THE MAJOR
MOTION PICTURE *SHOWGIRLS*
"Come back when you've fucked some of that baby
fat off."

A PERFECT MATCH
There once was a boy named Blue
who lived in a very old shoe
he said the odor was foul
but he lived there somehow
what else is a young man to do?

There once a girl named Bridgett
Bridgett was a very small midget
I have found (because I looked around)
that Bridgett weighed less than two coffee
  grounds
and was no taller then my fifth digit.

I had to get these two together
for good or at least better
there had to be a way
but I don't think he'd get the time of day
because his shoe wasn't even made of leather.

68

So I told a little lie
cross my heart and hope to die
but this shouldn't double my trouble
because I'll pick up the rubble
of the "Whos" "Whats" and "Whys."

I told her Blue was a big cheese
and about how he liked to tease
that he lived in a loafer not fit for a penny
and there was not room for many
in his home nowhere near the seven seas.

I told Blue she was "petite"
and how her toes smelled very sweet
so if people start to stare
he really shouldn't care
because they're just looking at her very lovely
    feet.

So I made a reservation
at the nearest restaurant sensation
I knew there wasn't much Blue could afford
but thank the lord
he was the one-millionth customer at that food
    station.

But I was having my doubts
and the doubts were all about
how they would not get along

and thinking I was wrong
and hoping they would not fight and shout.

But I am very smart
I was right from the start
I'm not lying
sparks were flying
and I was just happy to play my part.
(in matters of the heart)

They are perfect for each other
and he'll never find another
who eats like a mouse
can fit in his small house
and takes care of him better than his own
  mother.

And it's hard being small
when you have it all
you find what you can (in your man)
Bridgett found someone to understand
someone who made her feel ten feet tall.

These two are my friends.
(And we're friends to the end.)

Sometimes do you feel you cannot remember the
present, while what happened yesterday is
crystal clear?

I'LL HAVE A DOUBLE
If you take a drink from the cup of life, then
I will take two. If you spread your pixie dust
across the party, then I will give it a happy
thought in which to fly. And if you kiss me
once and never again, I will accept half your
lips and nothing more.
Maybe the top one.

CHECKPOINT
So far I have written 9,578 words and 30,992
individual letter, not including this one.
(Make that 30,993 individual letters.) Are you
impressed???

It was perfect. It could not have gone better.
Everything was right. Nothing was wrong.
Everything worked. Even the things that work
only once a week fell right into place and
happened in such a way that I could not wish
for better. I was great. They were great. And
I didn't even ask for better than normal. It

happened without a word. It was beautiful. It felt right. It was perfect. And she loves me now. I think.

Set a place for me at the table. Make room on your mantel. Leave a glass of water by my bedside. I'll leave my jacket at the door. It is time to set aside things past. And never forget who we were before.

Masturbation is the sincerest form of flattery.

JUNIOR'S RELATIONSHIP HISTORY (in pictures)

!!! W A R N I N G !!!

The following is a work of fiction and
should be read as such. This is not to be
misinterpreted as an aggression or hatred
towards the feminine population or the pharma-
ceutical industry. The artist would also like
to add that axes are dangerous and should only
be used under proper supervision. Despite pop-
ular belief, the characters are not based on
real people. Your author would like to add
that he is not emotionally scarred.

Thank you for your time.

the adventures of deacon and mildred

this is deacon

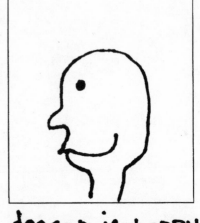

deacon is happy

this is mildred

mildred is not happy

look, deacon has a pretty flower

mildred does not have a pretty flower

mildred is crying

isn't that nice, deacon is giving mildred his flower

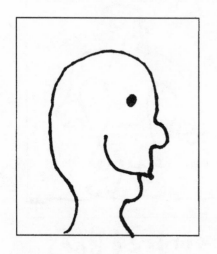

now mildred
is happy

mildred needs
her pills

I love you
mildred

JUNIOR'S (brief) DATING HISTORY IN WORDS
Who's that? Who the hell are you? Huge
erection. I want you. I want you. I want you.
What did you say? I wasn't listening. Do you
want some gum? You're doing it wrong. I want
you. What do you think you're doing? That's my
side of the bed. What's your name again? What
kind of clever scenario can I come up with to
figure that one out? I don't care. Why can't
she lie still? I'll be right back, I just
can't sleep. I could set the clock forward a
couple of hours, then she might just leave.
That's pretty funny actually. DING-DING-DING!
Time for breakfast. I hope she's not a picky
eater. Why won't she leave? See you later,
it's been fun. I'll call you (No I won't. No I
won't. No I won't.). Bye. Huge erection. Thank
god that's over.

Lonely Tony Masconi likes eating pepperoni
minestrone with Rice-A-Roni while fighting
Moses Maloney. He got a boney from Ms. Mary
Mahoney who showed him her best moany like a
phony bologna. They both got a little stoney,
and she rode his pretty pink pony because he
had a big screen Sony and she liked to watch
Home Aloney.

FREUD

Sometimes a cigar is just a dildo.

Pokey Poke.

DAD—PART 5

My father liked to hit things. His favorite
thing to hit was my mother. There were
constant screams of things like "Call the
police" and "I can't live like this." He
hurt her a lot. Once when I was seven or
eight my father, mother, and I were walking
down the street when an argument broke out.
Eventually my father got very angry and
began shamelessly beating my mother over the
head over and over again with his fist right
in front of everyone on the street. We were
beginning to draw a crowd. A brave young man
saw this and stepped forward. He tried to
say something but my father just threatened
to beat him like he was his wife. And the
young man, being young and having no vested
interest in my mother or me, declined the
fight. As he walked away he gave me a look
as if to say "Sorry, kid."

THINGS THAT ARE IMPORTANT (in no particular
order) . . .
Dad. Plastic. Television. People who build
things. People who do math. Oxygen. Concrete.
Comedians. People with strong fingers. Food.
Water. Music. Skin. Pillows. Toilets. People
who can take my abuse. People who abuse me.
Head scratchers. Solar panels. Bananas.
Carpenters. Lifeguards. Mud. Doorknobs.
Bathtubs. Soup. Soap. Turtles. Razor blades.
Boxes. People who work in box factories. Light
bulbs. Terry cloth. Mother. The sun. Rubber
trees. Trees in general. Doctors. Kittens.
Holding hands. Other displays of public affec-
tion. Women. Lobsters. Professional wrestling.
Pizza. Photographs (not photographers). People
who drink their own pee. The Discovery
Channel. Deep-sea divers. Astronauts. *The Mag-
ical Mystery Tour*. Fast food of any kind.
Electric cars. Death. Having time for others.
Having time for yourself. Alcohol. Meteor
showers. Videocassettes. Learning new things.
Working hard and being rewarded. Sushi.
Gargoyles. Vaseline. Friends. Making lists.
Making a gift for someone. Hairbrushes. Making
peace with your past. Honey bees. Mythology.
Tony Hawk. Paper.

POOR HEIDI

Heidi was her name. Hiding was her game. When
Heidi hid, horses halted, hotheaded hares
hopped hopelessly hither, and homeless
Harriets huddled over heaping helpings of hum-
mus. Heidi would huddle humbly, hoping her
hiding helped her hearing. For you see, Heidi
could not hear. Hearing was hard for Heidi.
Hiding helped Heidi's hearing. Until one day
hiding did not help Heidi's hearing. Heidi
hopped out of her home on a historically hot
day for hiding when Heidi's hunger for hiding
halted. How did it halt? For you see, Heidi
could not see anymore. Hiding helps little
when you cannot see whom you are hiding from.
Heidi is not here anymore.

i dont want to be crude. i dont mean to be. i
say things sometimes. i dont mean to. ive
regretted things. a great many things. i hope
i am not too different. i dont mean to be. ive

done things sometimes. things i wish i never
did. it sounds silly i know. why am i talking
to you about it? you dont understand. why say
anything at all? i dont mean to. i try too hard
sometimes. way too hard. i dont know why. its
not as easy at it seems. i dont mean to. it
sounds so different when you hear it. why did i
even think that? why do i think anything at
all? i think im going to be sick. i dont mean
to. i think i should go home. this is not my
kind of crowd. i should just stop. im taking up
too much time. whats the point. i dont mean to.
i wish it was easier. i wish a lot of things.
im really not feeling well. i dont know what to
do sometimes. sometimes i get better. i dont
mean to. but i am not sorry. this is not an
apology. but i forgive you for thinking that.
this is a confession. i didnt mean to.

will you see *me* to the door? will you see *me*
out of this place? i don't want to be here
anymore. will you show me out? i don't know
what i'm doing anymore. get me out of here.
show me the way out. do you know the way out of
here? please tell me. you told me you loved me.
is five minutes enough? enough for me to run
away? enough for me to explain myself? enough

to draw a meaningful conclusion about whether
or not you love me right? not for me so i
think i'll go. enough. so will you show me the
way out of you . . . i mean will you show me
the way out of this place that i dont want to
be anymore? kinda sorta lying. whatever. im
just drunk. show me the door.

                                                          odlm

work a little harder

I KNOW YOU DON'T LOVE ME

I know you don't love me but . . .
Can I sit in your chair?
It looks so comfortable way over there.
I won't break it I swear.
I just need a place to sit down in this hot
  winter air
So can I sit in your chair?

I know you don't love me but . . .
Can I read your book?
Can I take a look?
I've always wanted to learn how to cook.
I just needed a little hook.
So can I please take a look at your book?

I know you don't love me but . . .
Can I sleep in your bed?
Because you see, my bed is uh . . . dead.
I'll sleep at the foot, and you at the head.
It's good for the blood, or so I have read.
So can I sleep with you in your bed?

I know you don't love me but . . .
Will you dance with me?
Don't worry, no one will see.
I know the electric 1-2-3
So will you make me that lucky?
Will you give one little dance to me?

I know you don't love me but . . .
Will you hold my hand?
Just tell them I'm with the band.
It doesn't have to be grand.
Or I can just sit while you stand,
If you don't want to hold my hand

I know you don't love me but . . .
Can we be together?
And I don't mean forever.
It's just that now is slowly becoming never.
And I don't want to be without,
When it's time to go to the place that is better
So can we be together?

I know you don't love me but . . .
I love you.

the end . . .

blank

THE END.

part three

isolation

When I was young, like three or four years old, my parents got mad at me for something I probably deserved. I remember crawling under my blanket and thinking I would never ever come out from under it. In the moments following, my future flashed across my young eyes. I saw myself eating under there and sleeping. I saw myself growing old with a long beard. I envisioned almost everything logistically except how to go to the bathroom, but I felt that that was something that could be worked out.

I can't remember how long I stayed under there, but I do remember being coaxed out by the proposition of dinner. But I often wonder if I should have stayed there.

correspondence.

Junior has run away. He is hurt and he is
scared and so he runs. It's all he knows. He
doesn't know where he is going or where he's
been. He has already forgotten where he is.

The following is a series of letters written
by Junior while in exile. He wrote them all
and put them into envelopes and into the
pocket of his suitcase where he kept things
like that. He had no intention of sending any
of them.

You may be asking yourself why, if he had no
intention of sending them, he would publish
them in a book for the whole world to see.
The answer is quite simple. Junior thought
that this very public way of displaying his
extremely private emotions was the only way to
make himself feel better about writing them in
the first place. Plus, he's a hypocrite.

Take them for what they are.

Enjoy.

A LETTER TO DAD

Dear Dad,

So . . .

Dear ███████,

First and foremost, I'm alive. Isn't that nice to hear? I'll say it again: I'm alive.

I'm sorry I left so abruptly and without saying a word, but it had to be done. I can't really talk about it now. It's not that I can't, I just don't want to. Fucking women. I just had to go and I'm sure you can tell from the postmark that I'm not in Kansas anymore.

But I'm having fun, if that means anything at all. I'm seeing the world on my own terms as opposed to how I want to see it, and that's a big difference. I thought I'd meet more foreign girls out here, ones who don't speak English and are well-versed in the language of love. But it's funny, the only ones I end up talking to are Americans. And they're much more bold out here, like they feel like they can say and do anything they want because they're so far away from home. Do you want to hear the best pick-up line I ever heard? "Nice shoes, wanna fuck?" I swear to god this girl walked right up to me and said that. And we had fun too. But like I said before, that barely means anything at all. Having fun and being happy are two totally different things.

But these sexual conquests only mean so

97

much. I think I have a newfound confidence in my abilities, but I take that for what it is. There comes a time in every man's (woman's) life when he (she) must comes to terms with his (her) penis (vagina) and I think I've done just that. But that is all. Once again I take it for what it is.

I'm glad that I have this time for myself. There was so much going on at home that I felt like I was choking. Sometimes I'm like an ice cube sitting in a warm glass of lemonade. Sometimes I can feel the outside trying to make me melt. One second I was in the ice tray with all my fellow cubes and the next thing I know I'm in someone's drink trying my best to survive. And there I am. Just there. Slowly melting away. Never being noticed. Helplessly watching myself be consumed. God I wish I were a popsicle, because they have much more fun. Even ice cubes need a vacation and so do I.

I'm gonna go now. I'm going to live a little more so I'll have more stuff to write to you in the future. I hope this letter finds you well, but don't write me back, because by the time it reaches me I will have moved on.

With love,
Junior

p.s. Don't tell anyone about this letter. If
they know you received it they are going to
want one of their own and the next thing I
know I'll be writing letters all day.

MESSAGE IN A BOTTLE

Captain's Log:
Day 162 of exile
06hr 52mn

Nights are getting dull. Stop

Cannot sleep at night. Stop

Drugs to help me fall asleep. Stop

Ran out of hash yesterday. Stop

I smoked the last of the roaches in the safe.
Stop

I am at my wits' end. head explode. Stop

If you find that note amongst the waves please
send help. Stop

Or hash. Stop

Or head explode. Stop

The Wembling Warrior

THE FOLLOWING IS A NOTE WRITTEN FOR A YOUNG
WOMAN FROM ARGENTINA UPON HER REQUEST.

Why won't she kiss me? Why won't she leave?
Why is she eating my jelly beans? Why is she
asking me what I want on my omelet? Why can't
she understand? Why can't she speak English?
Why is she wearing that much eye makeup? Why
is she wearing that much eye makeup and
not kissing me? Are they all this stupid
in Argentina? She thinks too highly of
herself. She doesn't want to be in my book.
Her name, in my book. Too bad for her. She
just won't kiss me, and damned if she wants
to leave.

SHE DIDN'T LIKE IT.

A LETTER TO DAD (Attempt #2)

Dear Dad,
        What's going on? How's it hanging?
How've you been? Where you at? And say hello
to the little lady.

        By the way, happy new year, happy
belated birthday, happy St. Patrick's day,
happy Easter, happy Valentine's day, happy
Chanukah.

        That's great. Nice to hear. I hope so.
Just one for me please. Thank you. Bless you.
You're welcome.

        Well, time to get moving. Gotta stay
ahead of the traffic. I've got things to do
and people to see. Defiantly. I'm a very busy
man. We'll talk about that later. Where'd I
put my jacket? Gotta go.

THE WEMBLING WARRIOR PART 9,999

A LETTER TO BRITNEY SPEARS

dear britney spears,

do you like chocolate? I love baby one more time.

~~████~~

boom boom bang boom boom bang. Singing is like chocolate.

love,
WW

A LETTER TO DAD (Attempt #3)

Dea

GREETINGS FROM MAUI

To Whom It May Concern,

It is my duty to regretfully inform you that the man known as Oscar de la Mancha, who was reported missing twelve months ago and was last seen walking the beaches of Maui wearing a straw hat and mumbling incoherently, has been officially declared deceased. It is the policy of the Hawaiian state police to presume missing persons as such after the period of one year.

Preparations on behalf of the family have already begun and, pending a final report, the deceased's personal items will be transported to this address.

If you would like to file a grievance, or simply think young Oscar has fallen off the face of the earth, please contact Detective P. Dondo Nuts of the Hawaiian state police.

We would like to express our deepest regrets for your loss. We extend our deepest sympathies. Our regards to the bereaved. Sorry.

Signed,
The Hawaiian State Police Department

DEAR FATHER

Dear Father,

Long time no speak . . . well, this
isn't exactly speaking, but for both of our
sakes it will have to do.

This is just about the end of the book
and I know you probably disapprove. I never
expected you to like it. This was never a part
of your vision, whatever that was. You never
decided to let us in on it. Sometimes I wish
you had.

It didn't have to be like this. It
shouldn't be this way. We could have stayed
poor. Since we last saw each other I have read
a lot about families and about how they can be
happy with what they are. Is that true, or am
I crazy?

I am happy with where I am. Wouldn't
it be great if we could just be happy for
each other? But we're not. You might even
write some angry letters to that effect. I
might even read them, if I didn't already
know what they said. Nothing surprises me
anymore. I have less and less fear every day.
Thank you.

You showed me fear. You showed me what
it was like to be afraid. You gave me fear. I
saw your sadness. I now know madness. My skin
gets thicker every day. The winters are not as

cold anymore. I have learned from you. I am no longer a child.

You hurt people a lot, you know. I am not just talking about your family and the other important people around you; you hurt our name. I should know. Did you know I had to apologize on your behalf way too many times? I'm not talking about ten years ago, I'm talking about right now. The sins of the father have been passed on to the son. I had to say "I'm sorry" for someone who was always too afraid to say it himself. I'm sorry for that.

You made a lot of people cry. You made my mother cry. As time went on I used to tell you some of the horrible things you did to the people you were supposed to love. I would tell you why I was so angry with you and why people hated you so. Then you would laugh and tell me that you didn't remember those things and how they hadn't happened.

That used to get me angry most of all. I was in a rage for many years knowing that you did these things to me and my family and how you would sleep comfortably at night thinking you were a good person. Thinking that I was just making it up to be dramatic.

The saddest thing was that when I got older I realized that you might not be lying. You might have actually thought that you never

did those things, that you never hurt me.
You did.

But I'm past the point of reminding you
and myself about the way things used to be.
I'm not going to hang on to the past like it
owes me something. I wasn't trying to call
you out on anything, I just wanted you to
remember. I want you to see these things and
know that you were the man that did them. I'm
sorry I had to do it like this, but it wasn't
for your benefit. Nothing is anymore. I'm
sorry.

I'm sorry things turned out the way they
did. I'm sorry I wasn't better. I'm sorry that
you doubted me when you did. I'm sorry we
started out so poor. I'm sorry the world swal-
lowed you up. I'm sorry that you never got
through to me. I'm sorry that you hated
anything at all. I'm sorry that you made me
fish when I was sick. I'm sorry that I didn't
enjoy fishing as much as you would have liked.
I'm sorry if I've embarrassed you. That was
never my intention. I'm sorry for what you did
to your wife. I'm sorry you couldn't tell anyone about how you felt. I'm sorry for the way
you spoke to me. I'm sorry that you felt you
had to hide. I'm sorry for never being good
enough. I'm sorry you never felt the need to

right all the wrongs in your life. I'm sorry
for everything.

But that is the extent of my sorrow.
You've done too much for anyone to ignore, especially me. I've stopped trying. I've only
accepted. I'm smarter than that, I'm smarter
than you remember. I don't need you to teach
me any more lessons.

Lesson learned. You taught me how I
never want to be with my children. You taught
me how I never want to be with women. I've
never hit a woman. I pushed a girl once. I
pushed her a little harder then I would have
liked. I was so ashamed I locked myself in a
room for a week. I couldn't look at her. Isn't
that funny? Thank you.

You taught me about anger and rage. You
taught me how to retreat. You unwittingly
taught me how to find my own world, how to
live in my head. You taught me that there were
some things not worth fighting for. You taught
me how life can fall apart. You never showed
me how to put it together again. I'm teaching
myself now. And no, I still won't fight you.

I am no longer angry with you. I hope
you don't hate me. I am strong. I am healthy.

I am going to make mistakes. I am going to apologize.

I am my father's son. I am Junior.

                                    Your son.

A LETTER TO THE READER

REASONS I DON'T NORMALLY WRITE LETTERS
(in no particular order) . . .
Dad. They never say what I want them to say.
They take too long to write. They get
misinterpreted (at least in my case). They can
mean too much to people. I don't know how to
make them sound the way my lawyer's do. I
don't read my mail. I don't spell very well. I
think faster than I write. I'd rather call the
person. Sometimes I don't have enough to say
to a person to fill an entire page. Postcards
are not private. You get no immediate reply.
Sometimes you get no reply at all. I never
really feel like I'm saying what I really want
the reader to hear. Someone other then the in-
tended recipient could read it. Someone might
laugh at it. It could get lost in the mail and
all your hard work could be in vain. I'm too
lazy to go out and buy stamps. People won't
appreciate what I am saying to them when it's
not coming out of my mouth. They prove my the-
ory that I'm a hypocrite. I hate letters.

Dear Mom,

I don't want you to feel left out of
this mess, so I decided to write you a letter
I have no intention of sending.

How ya doing? I'm sorry we've lost touch
over the last couple of years, but I think you
always knew I was the independent one. We
haven't talked much in the last couple of
years. Time only makes it harder for me to say
what I'm really thinking. I don't mean to
apologize, but I'm sorry.

Did you know I used to blame you? I
blamed you for a lot of what he did. I wanted
to see you protect yourself. I wanted to see
you run away with us and make it better. You
did make it better.

You might have thought, at some point or
another, that I didn't love you. I didn't feel
like I was your son. I felt like an orphan. I
felt as though I didn't have a family. I
didn't have you. I needed time to figure out
who I was, otherwise who would you be talking
to? How can you love me if I don't love
myself, not saying that I do. I won't forget
the past.

But things are different now. Things
have changed and so have I. We don't have to

add water to the ketchup to make it last just that much longer. We don't have anything to hold us back. I don't want to try too hard.

So now that we're starting over, where do I begin? The beginning is always the hardest part of any story . . .

the end . . .

blank

THE END.

part four

junior's blue period

As you may or may not have noticed
(depending on the severity of your color
blindness), everything you are reading on this
page and the following pages is blue (except
for those other pages . . . where there's a
bit of red). Well, you are all lucky people.
You are all lucky-lucky people. All of you
have a front-row seat to the nether regions of
the human soul. You get to see with your own
eyes the sadness caused by the uncertainty,

119

comfort, and indecisiveness in one's life. We will revel in the . . .

To be perfectly honest with you, Junior doesn't truly know what a blue period is. No one has sat him down and told him what that actually means. He never took a class about it and has never read it in anything he's ever been exposed to. It's not that he doesn't want to know what a blue period is, he just hasn't gotten around to it yet.

He's just lost and tired and drinking more than he's used to. He is confused and scared and he put it all on paper.

Enjoy.

punchline.

THE JOKE KING
I am a joke. Am I a joke? Am I joking? Am I
Joe King? I am Joe King. I am a joke king. Am
I a joke king? I am joking.

BECAUSE OF NEGOTIATIONS FOR THE FILM RIGHTS TO
THIS STORY, TITLED "STEWIE'S PROBLEM," ONLY
HALF OF CHAPTER 11 CAN BE SHOWN TO YOU AT
THIS TIME.

. . . Helen entered through the front door with
Stewie by her side. He was now bandaged with a
bloody piece of toilet paper in his nose.

"Go upstairs and play in your room. I'll
call you if I need you."

Stewie nodded and proceeded up the stairs.
Helen swiftly moved to the living room where her
husband was sitting, clearly in the middle of
his ritual.

"Do you know what I just heard?" she said.

"Yes dear?" Clark replied, not looking up
from his paper.

"Stewie's doing it again."

"What?" said Clark with as much interest as before. To his credit he removed the pipe from his mouth this time.

"Take your shoes off if you're going to put your feet on the ottoman," she said with the authority of a mother.

Clark, without taking his eyes off of it, folded over the corner of the newspaper and addressed his wife. "I work hard for this house. These shoes get me to and from the place where I get our money. Without them I would look pretty silly in front of my boss and miss out on that big promotion. They deserve as much respect as me."

"What are you talking about?" Helen said, a bit agitated.

Clark put down the paper and calmly emptied his pipe into the ashtray. He composed himself and began to speak. "I'm talking about the fact that I come home from a long day of work and I sit in my chair and I smoke my pipe and I drink my drink. I do this every day. I've done this every day for the last eight years. We have a deal. Unless it's important you don't disturb me until seven thirty. You remember this. You remember it because I remember it."

There is a tense moment. What does she do now? Silence ensues. The battle is on.

"Just take your shoes off. Unless you want to clean the furniture off later."

"Just have Carmelita clean it later."

"She's the nanny, not the housekeeper. You don't believe in housekeepers because your mother didn't."

"Leave my mother out of this. And is this why you came in here, to bug me about my shoes, or is this just your way of asking for a maid?"

"I came in here to talk to you about something important, but now I just want you to take off your shoes. I just simply can't talk to you when you're like this," Helen said, rubbing her temples.

"Like what?" he replied.

"When you're in this mood where you're sitting in *your* chair and acting like the world, and especially I, owe you something. Can you just come out of your cave and talk to me for a second?"

"You are such a woman."

"What's that supposed to mean?" she said, now getting wound up.

"Nothing. Just tell me what you came here to say," he said, changing gears.

"Take your shoes off."

"It's cold."

"Then put your slippers on."

125

He goes to pick up his paper. A pause.

"I came here to talk to you about your son, because he's having a problem. I came here to see if you wanted to help. And I'm sorry this interferes with your ritual, and the least you can do is take off your goddamn shoes and listen!" Helen yelled for what might have been the first time in her life. She was surprised, but not as much as Clark.

Flustered, Clark righted himself. He took his feet off the ottoman and slipped his loafers off. Helen flipped her hair. A small victory, one of what she hopes will be many. Clark looks at his wife, a bit suspicious. "What's into you today? You don't seem like yourself."

"That's not important, your son is important. I just got back from the school. I had a meeting with Stewie's teacher and I . . . are you listening?" she said, just making sure.

"Yeah, I'm with you." Clearly he was.

"Stewie's doing it again."

"Doing what?"

"It." She nodded her head for emphasis.

"I'm sorry dear, but I have no idea what you're talking about." From the look on his face we know this to be true.

"Don't you ever listen to me? Am I just talking to myself sometimes?"

"Sorry. Geez, give me a second to catch up."

She brushed him off. "Whatever. Listen, Stewie got beat up at school today. It was that Stenson kid. He was bugging Stewie about the thing. This is the second time this month. I'm really getting worried."

"Oh," Clark said, now realizing. "He's doing that thing again?"

"Yeah. At first I said we should just let it go. It's just a phase. He's only seven and he'll grow out of it. But now he's doing it at school and getting picked on because of it."

"Uh-huh," Clark chimed in with an acknowledgment. Part sympathy for his son, part not.

Helen continued. "I've tried talking to him about it before, and Carmelita has too, but we just don't seem to be getting through to him. So I was hoping . . ."

"Uh huh."

"I was hoping you could talk to him about his thing."

Clark shifted in his seat, uncomfortable with her plan. "Are you sure that's a good idea?"

"Of course I am. You're his father. Like I said, I tried everything. I even had the school's counselor say something, but nothing has changed. He just won't stop."

"All right, I'll do it after dinner." He went to pick up his scotch.

"That's not good enough. I think you should talk to him now. He's pretty beat up and I think it would be good for him to have a word with his father. I'll go get him now." And before Clark could say anything back, she was gone.

Clark was almost in shock. What had gotten into her today? He began preparing himself for his impending conversation. He sat up in his chair but then leaned back down, trying new positions to see which would be most appropriate. Giving up, he picked up his drink and took a big sip. He walked over to the desk and took a seat. Getting anxious, he began sifting through some papers. Just then Helen returned with Stewie, still with the toilet paper in his nose, by her side.

"Stewie, Daddy needs to talk to you for a while. You be good and listen to him. I'll be in the kitchen if you need me." She then kissed her son on the head and whisked out of the room with a hint of a smile on her lips.

Stewie stood in the doorway for a moment, ignoring his father. He then walked over to the sofa and plopped down. He was so small that his legs dangled off the edge. Clark drank the last of his scotch. He hesitated but eventually made his way to the sofa and sat down next to Stewie.

There were a good two or three feet of separation between the two.

"So . . . buddy . . ." Clark said, starting the conversation, "what happened at school today?"

"Nothing," Stewie said, swinging his legs off the side of the sofa.

"That's not what I heard. What's this?" Clark pointed to the toilet paper in Stewie's nose.

"Nothing."

"Do you mind if I check your nose?"

"Fine."

Clark moved for the tissue and Stewie flinched. "It won't hurt, I promise."

"Okay," Stewie said, his face preparing for the worst.

Clark gently removed the tissue and inspected the nose. "It doesn't seem so bad. It looks like it stopped bleeding. How does it feel?"

"Fine."

"I shoulda seen the other guy, right?" Stewie didn't react to his father's attempt at humor. Clark tossed the toilet paper onto the coffee table. "How did it happen?"

"Steve Stenson did it."

"Why would he do that?"

"I don't know," Stewie said, turning his head away. "No reason."

"That doesn't seem right. People don't just hit other people for no reason. Did you say something that would make him do that?"

"No." Stewie began playing with his fingers.

"Then what did you do?"

"Nothing."

There was a long pause where Clark didn't know what to say. "Were you talking to Arthur?"

Stewie quickly turned and looked at his father for the first time. "What do you know?"

"I know you talk to him every day. I know your mother and Carmelita and the school counselor have talked to you about it and told you that you should stop."

"But he doesn't have any other friends. I don't have anyone else to talk to."

"You can talk to me."

Stewie shook his head. "You're always working."

Clark inched closer to his son. "I know you think I might be too busy sometimes, but I always have time if you need to talk or hang out."

"You're just saying that to get me to stop talking to Arthur."

"No I'm not. I'm serious. I know it might look like I'm too busy sometimes, and I might

not always come to you when I should, but that's
because I love you and I work hard so you can
have a good life. Do you understand?"

"Yeah," Stewie said halfheartedly.

"If I don't work, I don't get money to buy
your toys. You know?"

"Yeah, I do."

"So listen, let's make a deal. We can
shake on it and everything. Okay?"

Stewie turned to his father. "Okay."

"Okay, here's the deal. Any time you feel
lonely or bored or you just want to talk, you
can come to me. Okay? Any time you feel like
talking to Arthur, you talk to me first. Deal?"
Clark extended his hand.

"Anytime? Even after work?"

"Yeah, even after work."

Stewie thought long and hard on this for a
long time. He looked at his dad like a poker
player trying to weigh his bets. "Deal."

They shook hands.

"But you have to promise me, no more
Arthur. You can't talk to him at school or at
home or anywhere. Understood?"

"Understood." They stopped shaking and
settled in.

"So if that's it, maybe you should clean
up before dinner." Clark got up and began
walking over to the desk.

"Can I talk to him one last time?"

Clark stopped and turned to his son.
"What?"

"Can I talk to him one more time? Just to say good-bye." Stewie looked at his father with his big brown eyes, a look even the sternest of fathers could not refuse.

Clark pondered this for a moment. "Fine. But don't tell your mother I'm letting you do this. Okay?"

"Okay." Stewie got up and walked to the sliding door that led to the backyard. He slided it open and before he exited, he turned to his father.

"Bye."

"Bye."

Stewie exited to the backyard, leaving the door open behind him. Clark walked over to the door, waited a moment, and closed it.

The end of the world is coming
And
I'm going to have unfinished business

Am I beating the clock?

I am not, nor have I ever been, a member of the communist party.

I AM NOT SPECIAL
I am not special.

You know something about yourself you're not telling me. Only the coolest people have their secrets. But not me. Oh no. Haven't you heard, I am not special. I have no secrets.

Some things are beautiful and I don't know why. It scares me to no end. I know a girl who tells a great story without saying a word. I love her and she is my friend. I love her. She lives in my glass box. Have you ever closed your eyes? And like most people I say things for different reasons. I don't know why. I can say everything's not okay but the drama is just an attempt to be something and a way to say something so a silence does not make everyone run away. Especially her. I don't know what I'm doing, but that doesn't make me special. In fact, I am not.

I try to be unique. I don't know why. We think a finger is going to be pointed at us and all the things we want and expected will happen. Besides, we deserve it. No one wants to be a face in a crowd of normals. Everyone wants a voice. What's your frequency? We all think our dreams are unique. Mine are special. Not really.

Hard work pays off in the end, that's what they say. But it doesn't. Not always. And we try and we settle and we think about how life could be and how (if you had the time) you could paint that picture, or build that boat, or maybe play that piano at a dinner party. But nothing is enough. Not even my words, they are not special.

I sit and wonder to myself if any of what I do in my life is working, or worth it, or just not all there. If that means anything, as in nothing. Some things are harder than they look. Some things are just hard. Some things are not easy. I am not special.

I just said something new to you and you're not surprised.

If today be the day that I die, then tomorrow
is just another day I will never see.

PEOPLE WHO ARE DEAD (in no particular
order) . . .

Dad. George Washington. Ted Bundy. Frank
Sinatra. Sonny Bono. Mother Teresa. Jesus.
Princess Diana. Jack the Ripper. F.D.R.
Jeffrey Dahmer. Elvis? Babe Ruth. John Lennon.
Hitler. Zeus. Albert Einstein. Owen Hart. Jim
Morrison. Julius Caesar. William Shakespeare.
Jimi Hendrix. Genghis Khan. Audrey Hepburn.
Ray Charles. Buddy Hackett. Richard Nixon.
Wilt Chamberlain. John Candy. Duke Ellington.
Henry Miller. Abraham Lincoln. Bleeding Gums
Murphy. Mama Cass. Shakers. The local
shopkeep. Pablo Picasso. Karl Marx. J.F.K. Old
Yeller. Janis Joplin. George C. Scott. Stanley
Kubrick. Confucius. Leonardo da Vinci. Vincent
Vega. Nero. Bambi's mother. Groucho Marx.
Andre the Giant. Henry VIII. Johannes
Gutenberg. Dana Plato. Doc Holliday. Alexander
the Great. Joseph Stalin. Barry White. Divine.
Frederick Douglass. Martin Luther King.
Neanderthals. Socrates. Ray Combs. James Dean.
Thomas Jefferson. Louis Armstrong. River

135

Phoenix. James Joyce. John Belushi. Raul
Julia. Harry Houdini. Captain Marvel. Thomas
Edison. Plato. King Arthur. Robin Hood. Bobby
Phills. Jimmy Stewart. Derrick Thomas. Homer.
Montezuma. Mr. Bojangles. Moses. Joe DiMaggio.
Humphrey Bogart. Pierre Bonnard. Buster
Keaton. Thirteen Dalai Lamas. Kurt Cobain.
Walter Payton. Jackson Pollock. People who
caught the plague. Sid Vicious. Thomas Paine.
Cary Grant. Conrad McRae. Mae West. Andy
Warhol. Dwight Eisenhower. Freddie Mercury.
Marilyn Monroe. Sam Kinison. Mickey Mantle.
Name droppers. Helen Keller. Keith Moon.
Vincent van Gogh. Leopold and Lomb. Wolfgang
Amadeus Mozart. Joseph Heller. Al McGuire.
George Orwell. Heroes. Miles Davis. Phil Hart-
man. Spencer Tracy. Benjamin Franklin.
Geronimo. Minnesota Fats. Gandhi. Winston
Churchill. Natalie Wood. Christopher Columbus.
Tupac Shakur. Dante. Queen Victoria. Sammy
Davis Junior. Charlie Chaplin. Ivanhoe.
Notorious B.I.G. Billy the Kid. Chris Farley.
Moe Howard. Larry Fine. Curly Howard. And
sure, Shemp Howard too. Gilda Radner. Marco
Polo. Fred Astaire. Joan of Arc. Sigmund
Freud. Jackie Gleason. Isaac Newton. Lawrence
Olivier. Ferdinand Magellan. Bruce Lee. Red
Foxx. Charles Darwin. Herman Melville.

Rasputin. Theodore Roosevelt. Mark Antony.
Arthur Ashe. Joe Louis. Jim Henson. Grace
Kelly. Dean Martin. Sitting Bull. Jacques
Cousteau. John Denver. Edgar Allan Poe.
Millions of people named Joe. Dylan Thomas.
John Coltrane. Sylvia Plath. Mel Blanc.
Brandon Lee. Woodrow Wilson. Fats Domino.
Peter Finch. Napoleon. Lucille Ball.
Cleopatra. /

Like flies to wanton boys, these are the days
of our lives.

Thoughts of loneliness
Thoughts of home
Thoughts of things to come
Thoughts of something calm
Thoughts never to be
Thoughts I will never see
Something to hold on to
Something that makes me blue
Something to give to you
Something I was taught to do
I know how to fool myself.

HOW THE HUMBLE FOLK DO
Wishing wells
Well wishing folk
People who go fly-fishing
People who have pennies to burn
Wishing for fish
Fishing for pennies
There's a sunken treasure at the bottom of the
wishing well
Wishing well the people above
The fly-fishing folk who are now saving their
pennies in their loafers

Loafing around like the fish mean everything
to these folk
But the fish are long gone
And the folk are gone too
With no more wishes in their shoes

The television has just promised me that a
monkey will cure cancer.

CHECKPOINT
There are 12,250 words and 39,792 letters in
the English language.

SOMETHING I SAID TO A WAITER ONE TIME
Wine is wine is wine is wine is wine is wine.

SOMEPLACE WITH NO TOILET
hey. do you remember the time when I was talking and you were talking and we were talking
together and nobody was listening to our talking not even ourselves and the person outside
knew what we were doing and what we were talking about but didn't care and knocked on the
door anyway because he had to pee and our

talking stopped and you ran away but maybe you
thought that I was following you but I wasn't
I was just trying to take a left and you faked
me out and then you went to the bathroom again
to talk some more with someone else who wasn't
listening because it's so much easier when you
don't tell them what you are talking about and
it happens all the time so why not go forward
and smile and laugh that way that you do and
you know I watch you when you laugh and
telling jokes is fun when you are around so I
try to learn a new joke for you but I don't
think it's funny enough so I'll just go and be
quiet somewhere you won't see me but don't
worry I'll have my cell phone with me just to
see your name once in a while but you don't
call because talking can be hard sometimes and
maybe you don't want to so you have to leave
pieces of yourself to smile at and to talk to
me that way that you do but sometimes I don't
think I'm right and I get scared that we might
never talk again so I get sad sometimes when
I'm not happy but then I remember the time
when I was talking and you were talking and we
were talking together and I wasn't listening
and you weren't listening and we never tried
to stop So now I'll give you something
valuable and special for you to put on

yourself and maybe you might like it and want
to talk some more and maybe you might
understand every other word of mine as I try
to say something that you love and I think
that's a good start and maybe I hear your
words for the first time and I might be
different in that someplace with no toilet.

THE WEMBLING WARRIOR PART .16C
HOW TO SUCCEED IN THE GAME OF LIFE
Let me tell you something about Winners:
winners win, losers lose, and buckets of lard
jiggle when you golf while floating up the
Nile with nothing but your mind and a rubber
ducky for company. Think about it.

Sometimes I feel like a three-foot tall,
poverty-stricken, homosexual, handicapped,
fifty-year-old Muslim woman with A.I.D.S.

I am and I do.

IMAGINING THINGS
Imagine if I didn't flip things around . . .

Imagine if we'd never met. Imagine if that
happened. Imagine if you didn't try to scratch
my eyes out the first time we met. Imagine if
you didn't bite my hand when I was bathing
your sister. You were so protective of her
then. It's been nearly four years since you've
last seen her. I lost contact with her
parents. I hope she hasn't jumped out a
window. And the same goes for your brother.

Imagine if I didn't try to eat your head.
Imagine if the lop-eared bunny who thought he
was a cat didn't try to rape you. Harvey. That
was the name of the bunny who thought he was a
cat. He'd shit in the litter box if it was
clean enough, which it rarely was. Imagine if
I wasn't so lazy. Imagine if you had a clean
place to shit every time you went. Imagine if
you were still living on the streets. Imagine
if I were living on the streets for the first
time ever. What would you do? Where would you
sleep? Would you eat garbage? Good question,
Gus; yes. Yes I would eat garbage the very
first day, even if I wasn't hungry. That would
show them. That would show them all.

You know, I thought about running away from
home when I was twelve or thirteen. Imagine

142

if I had done that. But then I realized that
something like that could never happen. First
of all, I only had one friend I could run
to and his mother and my mother talked
regularly. And the second . . . I guess I was
too afraid to eat garbage. I was too afraid
to live in a box. I truly wouldn't have known
what to do. But to make myself feel better I
swore to myself that if my life at home got
any worse I would live in a box and eat
garbage.

Imagine if my father didn't leave when he
did. I could be writing my words on the city
sidewalks. I could've been one of those
people who try to etch their mark on the
world with a tiny piece of chalk. I could be
living in the streets using nothing but the
finest chalk and eating garbage. Imagine
that . . .

But my father did leave, so . . . ha. And I'm
not living on the streets, and you do have a
clean place to shit (at least when I get
around to it) so ha-ha-ha. And you weren't
raped by the lop-eared bunny who thought he
was a cat so hardy har har. And I did bathe
your sister and you bit my hand and I tried to
eat your head and you tried to claw my eyes

143

out and we have met. And you're right here on
my lap. Isn't life crazy?

Imagine if life wasn't so crazy.

WHERE THEY GO LA-LA
Drifting eyes
May fall upon you
Full of lies
And wheatgrass too
You know their words
Can't hold us down
We'll fly like birds
Until the snakes come back round

FOR ALL OF YOU WHO USE YOUR COMPUTER *WAY* TOO MUCH

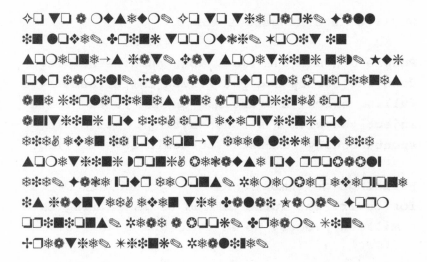

(Go to a museum. Go to the park. Fall in love. Drink
too much. Vomit in someone's hat. Eat something new.
Hug your family. Call all your old boyfriends and girl-
friends and apologize, for anything you did, for everything you did, even if you don't feel like you did
something wrong, because you probably did. Face your
demons. Remember everyone is haunted, even the Dalai
Lama. Form opinions. Read a book. Dream. Sin. Breathe.
Think. Realize.)

The world is in danger.

We live in a dangerous world.

People die all the time. You could be walking down the street and get struck in the head by a falling brick. A crazy man on the subway could inject you with a strange syringe. You could spontaneously combust. You could live in Iraq.

Buildings go tumbling to the ground and we run for cover. The world around us is falling into a million pieces. We are all going to die.

Who wants ice cream?

Wouldn't it be nice to have a place in the country like we talked about?

Cancer.

boat.

Junior.

WALKING SOLDIERS
Walking for days. I see people walking for days every day. I watch my television. I know what's

going on in the world. I see people walking.
Walking all the time trying to find where they
are going. Do you see them? Walking desperately
because they don't know what else to do. If all
else fails, walk. Walk 'til your legs are
tired. Walk on, dear soldiers of the masses.
Walk until you find whatever it is you're looking for. If there is something to find. Find
it, dear people; find what it is. Do you walk?
How many times a day do you hear that question?

  Wishes for things
Thankful for things
       Wishing for wings
  Pining for kings
         Thinking I have
wings
      Trying different
things

I must write what I know
. . .
exciting
I feel guilty not doing anything productive
I feel wrong about my guilty
Show me the time of day
Tell me im not wasting time
Ring ring
Just kidding

Why wont my phone ring
I am ruined
Hence I ruin things
He thinks im imagining things
(Hhe) thinks there's something wrong with me
Telepathically
5000 miles away
maybe there is
I haven't told you anything
And I probably wont
At least not for a while
I have no trust
No faith in those around me
They'll turn on me if it comes down to it
Their future vs. my future
Blah blah blah
In brighter news my lawsuits have settled down
At least through christmas
I want to build a house in the country
A nice place in (connetictt) or (masssachuttsettes)
or upstate
Fresh air
Green leaves in the spring
privacy
Maybe gets some horses maybe
And after I do that
Im going to build a big stone wall around it
So no one can get in

And keep everyone else out
There will be no phones.

It is definitely time to take some more drugs.

I have a cup of pills in my closet that I keep
hidden away from the world. I think of taking
them when I'm feeling like I am now. When I feel
like I do now, I think of taking my cup of pills
I keep hidden away from the world. Sometimes
when I've had enough to drink I take them out of
their protective closet and let them roll around
my fingers. I sit and play and wonder if they
would roll around my stomach that way. I wonder
if my digestive system would roll the pills I
keep hidden away from the world the same way
they roll through my fingers. I think I'm
fooling myself. They think I'm a fool. But I
have my pills. No one can take them away from
me. If I need them they are there for me to play
with and for me to wonder. I wonder if I should
take them. If I could . . .
Not today though. I'm not that drunk yet.
Besides, I think I'd feel sorry for the girl
who sold them to me. She was only supposed to
sell me one packet, but I convinced her to

sell me four. She would probably feel
terrible. I couldn't do that to her. She would
be crushed and think it was all her fault and
some small part of her would convince the rest
of herself that she could have stopped me. But
she couldn't. I could cut my wrists. You're
supposed to do it long-ways, not slant-ways.
If you want to do it right, if you really want
the blood to flow. If you're really serious
about doing a thing like that. There's a
million ways to do it. I prefer my cup of
pills. I like them hidden away from the world.
For now that's my right way to do it.

punchline.

Sometimes I don't know if my life is a joke. I'm sure it is, especially when people are laughing. It's hard to know who you are and it's equally impossible to figure out what the rest of the world says about you when you're not around. People say things.

I could have done it to myself. I could have gone out there and made an ass of myself. I could have run with the wrong crowds. I could have been bitter and angry at the world because it owes me something. But it doesn't, and I'm not. But beyond that I have no control over what the world says about me or my book or anything else associated with me.

I just need to lighten up. Not everything in my life is crazy, just sometimes the crazy things happen all at once. I need to learn how to dance and sing and especially laugh without worrying what the world (myself included) thinks about it. I need to lighten up . . .

When I was growing up, my godfather spent a lot of time babysitting my siblings and me. One of the things he did to keep these energetic children entertained was tell us jokes. Some of them were funny and silly and some of them were plainly not suited for children of that age. But we enjoyed them and laughed whether we knew what they meant or not.

But occasionally he would test us and tell a joke that didn't make sense and wasn't funny at all, just to see what we were laughing at. If you were caught laughing at something you weren't supposed to, it was pointed out to the rest of the group and they took pleasure in ridiculing you for the rest of the day (or as long as their young brains could retain the information).

It's a game I still play to this day. You should try it at your next dinner party.

TEN BAD JOKES FROM A BOOK IN A GOODIE BAG I GOT AT A PARTY FOUR MONTHS AGO

1. Setup:
Which members of the orchestra can't you trust?
Punch line:
The fiddlers!

2. Setup:
Where do tadpoles go to change into frogs?
Punch line:
The croakroom!

3. Setup:
What do you get after it's been taken?
Punch line:
Your picture!

4. Setup:
What does the ocean say when it sees the coast?
Punch line:
Nothing, it just waves!

5. Setup:
What do you get from nervous cows?
Punch line:
Milk shakes!

6. Setup:
Which dog is the most expensive of all?
Punch line:
A deerhound!

7. Setup:
Who can shave three times a day and still have a beard?
Punch line:
A barber!

8. Setup:
Arthur, did you take a shower this morning?

Punch line:
Why . . . is there one missing?

9. Setup:
How do hens dance?
Punch line:
Chick to chick!

AND FINALLY . . .

10. Setup:
What has a bottom at the top?
Punch line:
(Drumroll please)
A leg!!!

the end . . .

blank

THE
END.

part five

the end that comes

right before the end.

It took me ten minutes to write this sentence.

THE
END.

at one point in my

life.

     If you could close your eyes and read
this at the same time I would advise you to do
so now. I would like for you to imagine a
young man sitting at his writing desk that he
romantically purchased from an antique store
because a French woman told him it was "the
kind of desk a person could reinvent himself
as a writer with." Now imagine this same young
man has just written the next great American
novel. What if he just wrote the most perfect
book known to humankind? What if it were

perfect in all its imperfections? What if it were as important, and sincere, and significant, and meaningful to the writer as it was to its audience? What if it said all the things you wanted to hear? What if he said all the things he wanted to say? What if it popped?

Now imagine that this seamless and flaw-less work of art that this naïve young writer has stumbled upon was missing one vital piece. What if it didn't have an ending? What if it did and it didn't? What if the words were there, with all the commas and sentences and what-have—yous, but there was no ending? What if it didn't even whimper? Imagine if your writer told you that there was no resolution to life and not everything makes sense in a way that you could put on paper? Would you feel gypped? What if he told you that writing an ending was too hard so he just whipped something together because he felt he had to? What if it wasn't any good? Would you forgive your writer? Would it ruin everything you read before it? Would you forgive the writer?

Now open your eyes. Is it clear to you? It is for me. Do you see where this path has led me? Do you see the pickle I'm in? I now

162

have to come up with a way to bring this all
together. I'm putting the pieces in the right
places so you feel something for the
characters. It has to make sense; this all has
to make sense. This is it, my one shot at
redemption. All my hard work could be in vain
if the story does not come together in a way
that makes everyone, or at least most of you,
happy. What's the point of reading this if you
didn't like it?

What are you walking away with? You had
to have learned something. I certainly didn't
do this for the dimes. I think it's expected
of me. Lord knows if I were to read a book
like this one I'd like the title character to
walk away with more than just writer's block.
I need to know something about myself I didn't
already know before: like who is Junior?

IMPORTANT THING JUNIOR HAS LEARNED ABOUT HIMSELF WHILE WRITING THIS BOOK #1

I AM NOT "THAT GUY"

Coming to terms is a phrase that is thrown around way too much these days and is certainly not one that applies in this case. This was not a story of a young man conquering fear or searching for the answer to why he gets sad sometimes. I did not do this to be normal and to make everyone understand and all those things that make it too easy to write a suitable ending. I don't consider myself that interesting. I wasn't trying to clear the record.

I know I don't want to be "that guy." You know the one I'm talking about. I don't want to be "that angry guy" who goes around blaming his father or some girl or anyone else because this happened or that happened long before I could identify the world for what it was. I am nobody's fault.

I am my own man. I go to the store, I buy a pack of cigarettes, I smoke myself to an early death. That's my choice.

IMPORTANT THING JUNIOR HAS LEARNED ABOUT HIMSELF WHILE WRITING THIS BOOK #2

JUNIOR CANNOT MAKE A DEADLINE

Throughout my many years of experience doing many different things, one thing is certain: I cannot make a deadline. Whether it be for school or for work or for anything else, especially when it comes to this very book.

Now if it were up to me (which it isn't), this book would have been completed more than a year ago. This book would have been as perfect as it is today if it weren't for those damned deadlines.

I guess I never learned to follow through with all the promises I've made. If you had met me anytime before this project was completed I would have told you that it was on the verge of being finished and you would have a copy on your desk first thing in the morning. And I wasn't lying either. I've been on the verge of finishing this for almost two years. I don't know why.

Now, I'm not telling you that this book has taught me the importance of deadlines and following through with my promises. I'm not saying I'm a better man. I'm merely pointing out the fact that I've learned something: I am a liar.

IMPORTANT THING JUNIOR HAS LEARNED ABOUT HIMSELF WHILE WRITING THIS BOOK #3

JUNIOR FEELS MUCH BETTER

They say writing your thoughts and feelings down is healthy and that everyone should do it. It's not good enough to simply know something about yourself, that things only become glaringly obvious when you see them staring back at you from a piece of paper. Self-enlightenment is free, but the paper costs $1.99.

This is not an affirmation. I'm not telling you that I'm better or that I like myself more now than I did before. I'm glad I did it.

So I learned some things, big deal. People learn things all the time without having to write a book about it. That doesn't mean I'm special. I still haven't answered anything. That's not why I started this. Why did I do this?

Maybe this is all about blame. I never really thought about it before, but this could all be about rage or revenge or hatred or any of the other emotions that I (at one point in my life) had grown to love. I could wrap my anger around myself like it was a blanket and miss it when it was gone. What if it was karma? Maybe I wanted to get back at everyone who ever made me cry and write for all the people who gave me a reason to never cry again.

Let's see a show of hands: How many of you out there think I have been exploiting my childhood tragedies and current traumas for the benefit of the literary world? And on that note: Who believes me?

What makes you think I didn't make all this up just to make you like me better? Would you hate me then? What if I did this just to make people angry? Did you buy it? Did you go along with it or did you give me a sad look and move on? I'm not trying to make anyone angry, I just want to be forgiven . . .

Forgiveness. That's much better than blame. Never mind what I said before. This is a book about forgiveness and acceptance and all that crap. What if I were looking for a way to forgive everyone? What if I want to be forgiven? What if I wanted it all behind me?

What if it's already there and I keep dredging it up because I like the abuse and self-sabotage? What if I like pain?

The truth is that I (at one point in my life) did go to a therapist and did ask to be normal like everyone else. Fifteen years old and very impressionable, I walked into his office, upon the suggestion of the people around me, for a simple interview and walked out with three appointments a week. Not a good sign. I went to him for the next year, talking and telling him about everything. About anything. He seemed to ask a lot of questions about my father for some odd reason. We went from my long childhood to my recent adult years without missing a beat. He was constantly taking notes; he'd do it all the time. I'd cry, and he'd take notes. I'd tell him about the time I almost shot my eye out with a BB gun and he'd take notes. I even told him about the time I split my pants in front of this girl I liked when I was eleven and he would laugh and begin jotting down more notes in his yellow notepad.

So after twelve or so months of this I got curious about what he thought of me and what kind of notes he had been taking all this time. I wanted to know if I was making progress. I figured that after a year of this I should be feeling normal any day now, and I wanted to be ready for it.

So during one of my more serious sessions I said to him, "I've been coming to you for almost a year now and I need to ask you something: What do you think of me? I know you're a shrink and all but I need your opinion. What progress am I making? What do I need to do? Tell me something about myself that I don't already know."

Then the good doctor looked at me with surprise, as if I were the first patient of his to ask those questions. He then turned his head towards his notepad and began sifting through a year's worth of my jabbering. He then told me, "You have abandonment issues, which lead to problems detaching from things you get emotionally involved with." He then went on to say, "You should begin writing lists to itemize and prioritize the things that mean something to you so you know what's most important. You should do one thing at a time and then move on, because you get in the unhealthy habit of

169

holding on too tightly to the things you
love."

So I sit and I think. I think and I
think and think. I digest everything he just
gave me and turn to him and say, "You know
what, doc, I think you're right. I think I
might have detachment issues. I might just
have a hard time letting go of the things I'm
done with. I'm going to run right home and
make those lists you told me about. I think
those are a good idea. Thank you. And by the
way, you're fired."

The then surprised doctor asked me why
and I told him that I was sorting out the
things that were most important and he wasn't
one of them. He asked me to reconsider, but
the thought never crossed my mind. He left me
a message months later to ask me how I was doing. I never returned his call.

What if the good doctor was right, what
if I'm having a hard time finishing the book
because I'm afraid of who I might be without
it? That would explain the seven endings. Is
this book just going to sit on a shelf and
collect dust while I think (or not think) of a
suitable ending that won't leave a big hole in
my stomach? There is too much for me to do and

170

to say and to have done to me to have this book mess everything up. I need to think of a way to make myself feel better about moving on. I need to know what else is out there. I need to know I'm not alone.

**THINGS TO DO BEFORE I DIE
CHECKLIST**

Fire my therapist   (✓)

Write a book   (✓)

Have a case heard before the
Supreme Court   ( )

Appear on *Sesame Street*   ( )

Be given a plaque somewhere
important   ( )

Earn an honorary degree at
a university   ( )

Become a U.N. goodwill ambassador   ( )

Build a boat   ( )

Go into outer space   ( )

Skydive   ( )

Patent something   ( )

Put a personal message on
a billboard in Times Square   ( )

Build a really neat sand castle
with a moat   ( )

Get a tattoo   ( )

Go to: Machu Picchu   ( )
       The Pyramids   ( )
       Taj Mahal   ( )
       Sydney Opera House   ( )
       Great Wall of China   ( )
       Africa   ( )
       Leaning Tower of Pisa   ( )
       Both poles   ( )
       Jerusalem   ( )
       Mt. Rushmore   (✓)
       Stonehenge   ( )
       All four oceans   ( )
       The top of Mt. Everest   ( )
       Hawaii   ( )

Have a pet monkey   ( )

Have no less than three kids   ( )

Make my own moonshine   ( )

173

Quit smoking   (✓)

Learn to cook   ( )

Give myself a Mohawk   ( )

Win a dance contest   ( )

Learn to sing   ( )

Do laundry   ( )

Teach some kind of class   ( )

Have dinner with royalty   ( )

Work for the C.I.A.   ( )

Find inner peace   ( )

Dance on a grave   ( )

Eat turtle soup   ( )

Protest something   ( )

Vote   ( )

Collect Social Security   ( )

Fake my own death   ( )

Buy a new computer   (✓)

Have a fancy dinner party   ( )

Go square dancing   ( )

Celebrate my 50th wedding anniversary   ( )

Pick up smoking again   (✓)

Learn to play the piano   ( )

Fight in a war   ( )

Bet on a horse race   ( )

Become a senator   ( )

Die at 27   ( )

Build a better mousetrap   ( )

Enter a pie-eating contest   ( )

175

Set a world record   ( )

Find God   ( )

Lose him again   ( )

Find buried treasure   ( )

Go on a blind date   ( )

Own a restaurant and name
it after a girl   ( )

Inherit something (other
than a disease)   ( )

Live in France   ( )

Catch a home-run ball   ( )

Earn a black belt   ( )

Own my own island   ( )

Climb a mountain   ( )

Start a religion   ( )

Rob a bank   ( )

Hit a bull's-eye ( )

Drive cross-country ( )

Go on a safari ( )

Swim the English Channel ( )

Be 100% happy with my life ( )

Build a real snowman ( )

Drive a racecar ( )

Get a driver's license ( )

Apologize to the girl I cheated on ( )

Languages to learn:

    French ( )
    Italian ( )
    Arabic ( )
    Russian ( )
    Japanese ( )
    Hebrew ( )
    English ( )
    Sign ( )
    Spanish ( )

Go around the world in
a hot-air balloon ( )

Pump my own gas ( )

Learn to tie my shoelaces
the right way ( )

Build a fire with no matches ( )

Own a house on a lake ( )

Win father of the year ( )

Blow something up ( )

Give a speech in public ( )

Have a painting of mine
displayed in a museum ( )

Learn to paint ( )

Get arrested (✓)

Start an animal rescue ( )

Explore an unknown cave ( )

Shoot a gun   (✓)

Appear in a rap video   ( )

Follow a rainbow to its end   ( )

Fall in love   (✓)

Get assassinated   ( )

Learn to use chopsticks   ( )

Have a highway named after me   ( )

Catch a leprechaun   ( )

Throw out the opening pitch
at a baseball game   (✓)

Win an Olympic gold medal   ( )

Save a group of children from
a burning bus   ( )

Learn the secret to eternal life   ( )

Learn to skip rocks   ( )

Build a tree house ( )

Swim with dolphins ( )

Change a light bulb ( )

Cure a disease ( )

Have my own Las Vegas cabaret act ( )

Ride a camel ( )

Join a biker gang ( )

Perform comedy on Johnny Carson ( )

Build a time machine ( )

Win a Nobel Prize ( )

Spontaneously combust ( )

Get abducted by aliens ( )

Have sex on an elevator ( )

Eat a bug ( )

Figure out how ducks travel ( )

Ride a bicycle built for two ( )

Maintain a garden ( )

Change my name ( )

Marry Elizabeth Taylor ( )

Divorce Elizabeth Taylor ( )

Have surgery ( )

Own and ride an elephant ( )

Become a lead singer in a band ( )

Make soap ( )

Win the lottery ( )

Win an Oscar ( )

Learn to take a compliment ( )

Make a deadline ( )

Make a list of things to do
before I die (✓)

181

There's my problem. Unless it's
entertaining, why would you care whether or
not I feel better about myself? What do those
things mean and why did I put them there? I
just like to twist the situation around to
make it all about me.

Me-me-me.

THE FOLLOWING IS THE END PORTION OF A ONE-MAN
SHOW PRODUCED IN N.Y.C. IN THE HOME OF JUNIOR
ON THE MORNING OF JANUARY THIRD BETWEEN THE
HOURS OF 12:32 AM AND 3:04 AM, TITLED *A*
CONVERSATION WITH OSCAR. IT WAS THE ONLY KNOWN
PRODUCTION.

CHARACTERS:
    JUNIOR, 22.
    OSCAR, Unknown.

SETTING:
    Apartment bathroom, late night/early
    morning, winter.

NOTES:
    The part of Oscar should be played as
    the voice of an older man. This
    character should never be seen.

OSCAR: What about me? What happened? Where did
I go? What was that all about?

    Would you think less of me if I told you
this entire book was written to impress a
girl? I was doing it for her and it ended up
being about me?

OSCAR: Well isn't that nice. Everything has
been wrapped up in a nice little package. And
you get to run around and write a book, and
look at where I am.

I don't know what you mean.

OSCAR: I'm in Hawaii.

That's not bad. I could have put you in
Siberia.

OSCAR: But I'm just here. It doesn't make
any sense. One second I'm pouring my heart
out and the next thing I know I'm on some
island.

You're better off there.

OSCAR: You're not getting off that easily. I
need to know.

Know what?

OSCAR: Why you put me somewhere you've never
been and in a place I know nothing about. Why
you're ashamed of me and suddenly feel the

need to put me somewhere that nobody can
see me.

What can I say to make you go away?

OSCAR: Can I ask one last thing? Did she kick
me when I was down? Did she see that I was in-
jured and go in for the kill? Did she mean
anything she said or did? Did I want to
believe her?

. . .

OSCAR: Was she real? Was any of it?

. . .

OSCAR: If I leave I might never come back.

I know.

I don't know what I'm doing. I never did.
I get lost in my own mind and forget things
that might be important someday. I make out-
rageous claims and say things that only make
sense to me. It doesn't matter who I hurt. I
lie and exaggerate and make things that only

last 'til morning. I think too much. I have exposed myself like a porn star and am now more self-aware than a beauty queen. I've done so little and yet I feel as though I've accomplished so much. I like to talk. If you talk long enough and loud enough you're eventually going to say something that will offend someone. I get lost sometimes. I lose sight and begin asking questions that have no answer because that must be entertainment. It's not why this happened. It's not about whether or not you liked it.

This was not done for money or for lust or even for anger. This is not art for art's sake or art for the sake of Junior (meaning me). We could argue over whether this is art at all.

I did not make a difference. I am no more important today then I was yesterday. I did not say anything unique. I never want to give you the impression that what I do is not worthy, I'm just afraid it's not. But I'm beyond that now. I am beyond a moral or resolution. I'm not even sure if I was the one who did all this. It wouldn't even matter what page you started on or where it ended or if I gave myself a proper chance to explain myself. None of this really matters.

Life goes on. Some things happen, and some things don't. It's not what you do, it's what you don't do that makes you a big bright shining star.

FINAL CHECKPOINT

This book contained 16,764 words and 62,693 individual letters. I have used the word "drinking" 23 times. The word "the" appears 882 times, not counting this one. The word "phony" shows up only once and I am proud to say I did not use the word "bitter" a single time if you don't count that one. The number of times I used "journal" or "diary" not counting this one: 0. I have the chance to say I love you six times.

the end . . .

blank

DEDICATIONS (in no particular order) . . .
FOR:

Dad. The cast of *Saved by the Bell*. Angelo.
K-frogg. Anne Robinson. The person who
invented room service. Henry Miller. Sabrina
the teenage witch. Matt Groening. Buddha.
Stew. *Robot Wars*. *Kenan and Kel*. Chess
players everywhere. Richard Nelson. The fine
people at WWE. All the girls I've loved
before. Blueberry white chocolate cheesecake.
Eleanor. Irene Jacob. Frederic Kanoute. *The
Jenny McCarthy Show*. David Bowie. Greg "the
Mosh" Mosher. The Talking Heads. Madeline
Potter. Mom. Shane. Cody. Kierry. Quinn.
Chris. Rory. Sandy. Mandy. Eva. Jenna.
Patrick. Heather. Brian. Becca. Sean. Hacker.
G-Bird. Don Hill's. Celine. Sega Dreamcast.
Brett. Michael. Emily. Ken. Jennifer. Paul.
John Coltrane. L'Wren. My monkey. The
Ramones. The Nelson sisters: Yvonne, Heather,
and Robin. Goose. Prince. Paris. All the
people who've been so supportive of me.
All the people who doubt every move I make.
People who make ashtrays in their arts and
crafts class. Musicians who still put their
music on vinyl. Shorty. Rob, and Kristin
Powers. NAtaLIE. People who leave me alone.
The designer of butterfly chairs. MarKo. The
American ninja. The good people at the John

190

Jamison import company. Albert. Mr. Potato
Head. The person who discovered red. Pixies
everywhere. Fire extinguishers. Monkey butt.
Fishermen. Superheroes. My maids (god bless
them). Seth. Chad. Poker players. Steve. My
cats. Light-up lawn gnomes. Crayons. Toilet
paper. Singing Christmas trees. Sim's deli.
Santa Claus. The Smurfs. Wilmer. Randy.
Fenton. Candle makers. Miss Piggy. People
who read this entire book without skipping
over anything. Chairs. People I forgot to
put on this list. Catnip. *Star Wars*. Turkey.
Audrey. Monsters. My Yankee cap. The
Beatles. Mila. Super Monkey Ball. Toejam and
Earl. People who work the night shift.
Goldfish. Patchwork.

DEDICATIONS (in no particular order) . . .
Continued . . .

NOT FOR:
Dad. MTV. People who stare. Prince Charles.
Fine Young Cannibals. Kid Chameleon. ████
████████ Ben Hur. Halo. Jane Austen.
School. Nicorette. Furniture. ███████████ .
████ Coolio. Award shows. People who march
in unison. People who are born into a
religion and never second-guess it. All of my
uninspiring English teachers. Nuclear

191

weapons. Stupid people who shoot other people in high schools. Bed bugs. My gym teachers (not you, Nick). People who make glue the old-fashioned way. Spiders. People who breed animals for racing. Monsters. The jerk who stole my cab this morning (you know who you are). Terrorists. People who ring my doorbell. Shopping malls. Hitler. People who don't appreciate snow. Jury duty. Places that are not well lit. The church. People who wear suits all the time. Girls who have boyfriends that are twenty years older than them. Tabloid photographers. People who can look at an orangutan and not smile. People who are afraid of wine. Giant sausages. Showoffs. Villains. Overly dramatic people. People who underestimate the danger of ladders. Pat Buchanan. People who save their toenail clippings. Killer bees. The person who keeps calling my house and hanging up. The kids who made fun of me in grade school. Blah blah blah. Seal clubbers. Night clubb██████████ ███nbers. People who have nothing to say about the world. People who are afraid to wear rhinestones. Ax murderers. White people with dreadlocks. Thomas Edison. Buttons. Clones.

DEDICATIONS
Continued . . .

This book is actually dedicated to me, without
whose continued love and support this could
not be possible.

Thank you.

AN EXCERPT FROM MY UNFINISHED MEMOIR. NEWLY
TITLED *THE LEGACY OF MONKEY-MONKEY BOY AND THE
HISTORY OF THE CIRCUS*

SCENE MISSING

Pg. 258

. . . so I ended up with a lot of time on my hands
and a lot to do.

I had to find something to do with my new free
time, so I started clearing out the back of my house
recently. My place is a mess and has been ever since I
moved in four or five years ago. I have no excuse, I just
never got around to cleaning it and have been avoiding
it from the beginning. I still have boxes in the back
room that haven't been unpacked from the last two
times I moved. I don't even know what's in them
anymore. I even have boxes from my mother's old place
after it burnt down. Who knew what kind of treasures
were waiting back there?

So the girlfriend, being either tired of my
laziness or just plain bored, made the decision to have
me begin sorting through my mess. I first started with
the garbage, ten bags in the first hour alone. Then I
went through the mystery boxes and found all sorts of
things. Pots and pans that I thought were lost forever.
There was a beautiful silver platter from Tiffany, still in
its original box. There were pictures and clothing and a

small pile of cat poo in the corner. There seemed to be a little bit of everything back there.

But in one box I found something particularly interesting. I found a scrapbook. I don't know who put it together or why it was in my house. It was filled with all kinds of news clippings and advertisements and a lot of other stuff from my circus days. It was fun and kind of nostalgic. I never had the chance to see those things when I was a kid because either they were hidden from me or I just didn't have the attention span when I was ten years old to read an entire article. So I went to my newly cleared-off desk and began to read. Everything was there. Interviews, paparazzi photos, reviews, my past, everything. There were things from my life I didn't even remember in there.

I cringed at some of the things I used to wear. What was I thinking? I laughed at some of the headlines. How many times can you incorporate the word "monkey" into a clever pun? "MONKEY BOY GETS INTO MONKEY BUSINESS" or "IT'S NO TIME FOR MONKEYING AROUND" were among my favorites.

As I turned the pages, one of the things I began to notice was how grim it became. In the beginning everything was so positive. People seemed to like me and the things I did. Everything was so promising and optimistic. Then it began to turn. People had something to say about everything in my life. And when there was nothing to talk about, they just made things up. It

195

didn't matter how old I was or what it did to those around me or what people were starting to believe; they just wanted to use me to sell magazines. I wasn't even sure what was true or not anymore. There was an article about an apparent kidnapping attempt. Whether it was true or not, it's pretty messed up. It put that bad taste right back in my mouth and reminded me why I walked away in the first place.

I was going to put the book down before I even finished, but the tiny therapist in my head told me to continue, so I did. This book was convincing me that there were no redeeming qualities about my former life and that if I ever thought about returning to the circus I was either crazy or self-destructive. Why did I want to remember any of this? Why would I even think about going back? Why did I have to clean up the back room?

My mind was spinning as I turned to the final page. And to my surprise there wasn't an article there or an interview or something from the tabloids about my apparent relationship with Raquel Welch. There was a picture of my grandmother smiling ear-to-ear and standing in her front yard with two strange girls that I had never seen before. I didn't know who they were. Below the picture was a tiny note. It read:

Dear Mildred,

Want to thank you for taking that picture with the girls. They can't wait to show their friends that they took a picture with the Monkey-Monkey Boy's grandmother. They are all going to be so jealous. We all enjoy watching him.

Thanks again.

Sincerely,
Beatrice

It took a while for all of this to process. I stared at that picture of my grandmother for a long time. She looked so happy. These kids probably came from two towns over to knock on her door and get that picture. I made her proud.

That silly picture changed my opinion of myself. I spent so many years of my life running away from that cursed boy and all the trouble he caused. I saw nothing but the bad in him and what he created, and I never took the time to see what he did for me. That picture made me want to have kids so they would grow up and have kids of their own so I could tell them all the neat stuff their grandfather did decades ago. I, for the first time in my life, felt I had a legacy beyond what the tabloids said or what people whispered behind my back. I felt proud.

SCENE MISSING

Pg. 264

As I stood backstage on the opening night of the London circus at what the press had dubbed my "come-

197

back" (although I preferred "return") my mind was swimming with how I ended up here, why my life has gone full circle.

Getting back into the three-ring business was harder than expected. I scared people. Most people think us circus types who grew up in that atmosphere are crazy. And for the most part that is true. They feel as though life gave us something and then took it away. My problem was I never felt that anything that was given to me was taken away. I took, my parents took, everyone took and took and took until there was nothing left. But everyone got something for their time. But because of certain circumstances and, well, genetics, people were afraid of me. I've been told on more than one occasion that I look too much like the Monkey-Monkey Boy. Isn't that funny? How can someone look too much like themself/themselves?

I was able to find some modest circus work 5,000 miles away so that if I stank, hopefully only a modest amount of stinkage would make it back home. I jumped on the opportunity to work with such a fine circus.

But with my nerves surging as I stood backstage, I began to remember all the reasons why I was there and why I wanted to "return." I loved the pressure. I loved knowing I had to deliver no matter how much sleep I had the night before or what mood I was in. I still had an itch that had to be scratched. I couldn't wait to savor it and get it over with all at the same time.

I wasn't to perform as the Monkey-Monkey Boy though, and I had this feeling I was going to disappoint people because of it. Although I think deep down inside they knew, as I did, that it wouldn't be the same. The times of Monkey-Monkey Boy standing on a bucket on one leg and clucking like a chicken are over and long behind me now. I couldn't do it even if I wanted to. And so what, anyway? I never cured cancer or did anything else that would warrant the kind of attention I received. I'm not saying I'm the kind of person who's going to sit here and say I wasn't worthy, no matter how true that might be. I just never asked for all that has happened to me and I've always tried to be humble about it. In fact, I still cluck like a chicken at dinner parties from time to time. It would almost be funny now, if it weren't half disturbing.

There was no telling what was going to happen the moment I set foot on that stage or anywhere else in my life. People were going to talk, speculate, and wonder what became of that Monkey-Monkey Boy. People are going to have their opinions and that's fine. Some people think that I'm a shattered person because of my past. Well, I just enjoy the cracks on the surface.

Curtain's up. Time to go. Don't wish me good luck; in the circus we say "break a leg."

The end . . .

thanks for reading . . .